THE LEGACY OF BLACKTHORN

During a stormy winter's night, Meirian Penlan travels by stage-coach to take up a mysterious post at Blackthorn Manor. Wild and remote, Blackthorn lies amongst the great meres of Lancashire, surrounded by long-held superstitions, tales of witchcraft and uncanny occurrences. Once there, Meirian is drawn into a web of scandal, deception, blackmail and tragedy. Discovering old love letters and a terrible secret, she risks everything to set right a dreadful wrong — and unravel the disappearance of Blackthorn's medieval jewels . . .

JUNE DAVIES

◆

THE LEGACY OF BLACKTHORN

Complete and Unabridged

LINFORD
Leicester

First published in Great Britain in 2009

First Linford Edition
published 2019

A catalogue record for this book is available
from the British Library.

ISBN 978–1–4448–3967–8

Published by
F. A. Thorpe (Publishing)
Anstey, Leicestershire

Set by Words & Graphics Ltd.
Anstey, Leicestershire
Printed and bound in Great Britain by
T. J. International Ltd., Padstow, Cornwall

This book is printed on acid-free paper

1

Autumnal sunlight glowed upon the ancient jewels and old gold, trickling through Meirian Penlan's slender fingers. The amethyst necklace had been at the heart of everything. *Was* at the heart of everything here at Blackthorn — and had been for centuries.

Turning from the mullioned window overlooking the woods, Meirian couldn't help but recall that even on her very first night beneath the roofs of the manor house, Cousin Hafwen's candle flame had lit upon the portrait while they'd climbed the stair, softly illuminating the amethyst necklace adorning the throat of the squire's lady. Meirian had paid scant attention. She'd been far too wet and cold after the hazardous journey from York. That bleakest of November days seemed so very, very, long ago now . . .

Since leaving York before first light, Meirian had sat almost motionless in the corner seat, her cold hands buried deep into the folds of her cloak as she stared from the stagecoach window. Caught up with doubts and apprehension about whatever may lay ahead, she had scarcely noticed the changing landscape. York's grandeur and elegant shops had been left far behind as the coach trundled across the two counties: through villages clustered around swift rivers; along narrow cobbled streets; past smoke-blackened chimneys, factories, mills and workshops until Lancashire's industrial towns finally gave way to desolate moors stretching away as far as the eye could see.

Rain was falling relentlessly. Borne down from bleak hills and driven by a biting easterly wind, it scourged a barren land where an occasional sorry hamlet, solitary cottage or sheep fold were the only sign of life. Meirian shuddered, as much from the chill loneliness within her as the harsh weather without. What on earth was she doing? *Should* she have remained in York? Where she at least had friends and the surroundings were familiar —

'Miss, do you want to borrow the pig for a bit?' asked the matronly woman seated in the opposite corner. 'You're not used to travelling by coach, are you? No, thought not! You've not got nearly enough clothes on for travelling — I've three skirts on under this coat — The draughts that whistle through these coaches are wicked. The fares they charge, you think they'd fix the roof, too. We're getting soaked to the skin as well as frozen stiff! Here, lass,' she finished, offering the flannel-wrapped bundle. 'You take it and get yourself warmed up.'

'Thanking you, ma'am! And you're right, this *is* my first time aboard the coach.' Meirian leaned forward to accept the small stone bottle filled with hot water. Her damp hands and feet were numb, and she gratefully pressed her palms around the comforting warmth of the stone pig. 'I had no idea what it would be like, nor how long the journey would take. Do you travel often?'

'Often enough. We make this trip three or four times a year to visit our lad. He's got his own haulage business in Lancaster. I'm Mavis Pickles, by the way.' She smiled, nodding toward the muffled-up man who'd fallen asleep minutes after the couple had boarded. 'This is my hub, Archie. Sleep on a washing line, can my Archie. Where are you going, lass?'

'I'm bound for a place called Blackthorn,' replied Meirian, after introducing herself. 'I'm not sure how far it is.'

'*Blackthorn?*' Mavis Pickles sucked on her teeth. 'I've not been that far across county myself, but I've heard tell of Blackthorn! It's away out in the middle of the meres somewhere, isn't it? As wild and cut off as anywhere can be! Whyever is a young lass all on her own going to a godforsaken spot like Blackthorn?'

'My mother's cousin is housekeeper at the manor house,' answered Meirian. 'I've got a place there.'

'In service?' queried Mrs Pickles, considering the young Welshwoman's gentle manners and soft, very proper way of speaking. The lass was plainly dressed, but quite well turned-out. 'Eee, I'd not have taken you for being in service!'

'Well, I'm not exactly. Wasn't. In York, that is. I've been looking after a family's children since they were infants. I hear there are no children at Blackthorn, so I'm not at all sure what I'll be doing there,' she confided, an anxious frown creasing her forehead. 'I'd written to Cousin Hafwen some while since, asking if there was any work at Blackthorn. She wrote back and said there wasn't. Then last month, right out of the blue, Hafwen wrote again to say the squire's widow wanted some extra help about the household. I was to write her a letter all about myself. So I did,' finished Meirian with a rueful smile. 'And here I am on my way!'

'With no notion what the position is about? By, that's a queer do, int it?' remarked Mrs Pickles, shaking her head. 'Mind, I've heard it's a heathen land out there amongst the meres. Not surprising that they do things in a peculiar fashion.'

Gradually, their conversation petered out and quiet settled inside the coach. The scream of the wind, endless battering of rain upon the roof and the rattle of wheels drummed loud in Meirian's ears as she turned her face once more to the window and stared out into the black night.

A distant baying of hounds roused her, and shielding her eyes from the blinding rain, Meirian peered out from the window. Some small distance ahead, a pinpoint of light was moving through the darkness, swinging as in signal from side to side.

'Meirian, can you see what's going on from your side?' asked Mavis Pickles in alarm. Unguarded coaches were easy pickings for footpads and highwaymen. 'Why are we stopping?'

'I can see the glow of a window ... And a man with a lantern,' she began, leaning out again as the driver brought the blowing horses to a halt close by a squat building.

'You'll not get more'n a mile further!' shouted the man, his florid face eerily illuminated as he held the lantern high. 'Road's flooded!'

'I've a lass aboard for the Royal Oak and a couple bound for Lancaster.'

'They'll not be going anywhere this night, nor for any time till the waters go down.'

The howling wind drowned out the rest of the men's deliberations, and Meirian drew back from the window in consternation. Her new mistress had been expecting her to arrive earlier that evening. Someone was to have met her at the Royal Oak, which was apparently the coaching inn nearest to the manor of Blackthorn.

'Well?' prompted Mavis Pickles agitatedly. 'What's happening?'

'Hmm? Oh, the man said the road is flooded. I think we must be at a tavern of some sort.' Jolted from her thoughts, Meirian looked out again. The wind nearly took her breath away, and the night was so dark that she couldn't even see the horses clearly or catch any glimpse at all of the two men. 'The driver must've gone inside with the landlord,' she went on, ducking back within the window. 'Do you know this place, Mrs Pickles?'

'We're likely stopped at Butcher's,' she considered. 'It's the only tavern this side of the river — and a low enough place it is, too. Coaches don't stop here. They go straight past and away over the river out to the Royal Oak. That's a proper coaching inn, y'see. Nice rooms and decent food. Archie and me have stayed there a couple of times.'

'The Royal Oak is where I'm to get

out. Is it far away?'

'Miles from here, lass! Even when you get across the river, it's still a fair few hours off. And the roads just get worse and worse.'

Meirian sat back, taking stock. There was nothing for her in York any longer. She had nowhere to go back to. So the last thing she wanted was to annoy the squire's widow at Blackthorn. From their correspondence, she certainly wasn't a woman to suffer fools gladly. It would've been bad enough that Meirian was hours late, but not to arrive at all and keep everyone waiting might well cost her new position.

The driver stuck his head in at the window, rivulets of rain streaming from the brim of his hat. 'This is as far as we go!' he bawled above the wind and rain. 'Landlord says the road's flooded.'

'How long will it be before the road is passable?' enquired Meirian.

'How should I know?' the driver said with a shrug. 'Depends on when God decides to stop the rain, dun't it?'

'But I was expected at Blackthorn this evening,' persisted Meirian desperately. 'Whatever are we to do?'

'Two choices. You can go back to York in the morning,' answered the driver, 'or stay put and wait out the flood, although you might have yourself a long wait. Blackthorn's famous for getting cut off by floods and snow.'

'My hub and me'll be coming back with you,' chipped in Mavis Pickles, leaning forward in her seat. 'Is there any chance of us getting a bed here and a hot meal?'

'It's just a tavern, missus. There's no rooms, nor proper stabling neither. But the landlord's opened up for us so we can get a drink, and he sez we're welcome to his fire for the night.'

'I'll settle for anywhere that's warm and dry,' sniffed Mrs Pickles, elbowing Archie sharply in the ribs to waken him. 'This coach leaks like a sieve.'

Meirian clambered from the stage-coach and followed them into the tavern. It was hardly bigger than a shippon, low-roofed and windowless, the only light emanating from the dying embers of a fire and the candle standing on one of the shelves. A coarse sheet of sacking hung across the far end, and the landlord emerged from behind it carrying a trencher piled with bread and cheese. From his unkempt appearance, he'd clearly been roused from sleep by the baying of his hounds, and was yawning noisily as he set the food onto a table before disappearing behind the curtain once more.

Meirian sat on one of the settles, the Pickleses taking the other while the driver stretched out in a high-backed chair next to the fire. She didn't need to count the coins in her purse to know she couldn't afford the coach fare back to York, nor rent for lodgings once she got there and was seeking employment.

Purchasing a mug of tea, which was stewed and bitter, together with a hunk of stale bread and cheese, Meirian ate slowly. What was she to do? It might be days — weeks, even — before the floodwater went down and the road opened again. An unpleasant sensation suddenly ran the length of her spine and she glanced up swiftly, catching the landlord's greedy eyes walking over her. She certainly couldn't stay here, not after Mr and Mrs Pickles and the coach driver left in the morning.

Her thoughts were poor company as, pulling her cloak tighter about her and using her carpetbag as a pillow, Meirian leaned against the settle-back and closed her eyes. Somehow she had to make her way to Blackthorn. Apart from everything else, the remote manor house was where her only living relative bided. Cousin Hafwen was all the family Meirian had left in the world.

★   ★   ★

She dozed fitfully, and it must've been the early hours when impatient thumping against the tavern's door awakened her. Shifting stiffly on the hard settle, Meirian was aware of the landlord shuffling out from behind the curtain, muttering curses as he dragged back the sturdy bolts and wrenched open the door. A broad-shouldered gentleman bowed his head to clear the lintel and strode inside, brining with him a swirl of rain and gusting wind that set the meagre fire guttering.

'You're exceptionally busy tonight, landlord!' he remarked wryly, narrowing his eyes to penetrate the tavern's gloom and making out four slumbering figures gathered around the hearth.

The landlord cleared his throat and spat into the dirty straw littering the tavern's floor. 'What'll I be getting you, sir?'

'I'm looking for a young woman. A Welshwoman,' he returned, removing his hat and sweeping rainwater from his brow. 'She should've been aboard the Lancaster coach and was to have alighted at the Royal Oak in Kirkgate.'

'Lancaster coach only got as far as here,' replied the landlord, scratching the greasy stubble on his chin. 'There was a young lass got off — '

'Over here!' Still drowsy, Meirian scrambled to her feet. 'That is, *I* was bound for the Royal Oak.'

'You're Miss Penlan?' He was across the floor in a couple of strides, taking her hand and inclining his head politely. 'I'm James Caunce of Blackthorn. I understand my mother has been in correspondence with you? Please, won't you sit down? Landlord! Two hot toddies over here, and make them good strong ones.' James Caunce drew a chair close to the settle, tossing his drenched hat and cloak across the small table standing alongside. 'Miss Penlan, my apologies for having kept you waiting. This is hardly a suitable establishment for a young lady travelling unaccompanied. As soon as my bailiff brought news the road was flooding, I realised you'd likely be stranded somewhere out here.'

'I very much regret not keeping my appointment with Mrs Caunce at Blackthorn manor house last evening,'

Meirian said at once, eyeing the pale-haired man cautiously. He seemed amiable enough, not angry at having been inconvenienced. 'The coach driver said he could go no further. He's returning to York in the morning.'

'There's little else he can do,' remarked James Caunce. 'This tavern is the last point before the road drops into the valley. Out at Blackthorn we're on higher ground, away beyond the valley on the far side of the hills. Floods this side of the river cut us off two or three times a year. However, being Welsh,' he added, smiling across at her as the surly landlord banged two steaming tankards down upon the table, 'you'll know as much about rain as we do.'

'A fair bit, I daresay.' She returned James Caunce's smile warily, immeasurably relieved she was not to be stranded at this dreadful place after all. 'Although it's ten years and more since I was last in Wales.'

'We've a long and arduous journey ahead of us, and you haven't touched

15

your toddy yet. You really should drink it, Miss Penlan,' he urged, stretching long legs out toward the mean fire and studying her pale, serious features in the half-light. 'How is it you've been so long from Wales? It is your home, I assume?'

'Yes. Well, it was,' replied Meirian, doing as she was bidden and gingerly raising the tankard to her lips, and gasping as the potent drink took her breath away. 'We lived in Conwy. My father was clerk to a firm of attorneys. When I was fifteen, I went into the household of Mr and Mrs Iwan Allen to care for their family. They had just the four children then, all still quite young. At first, I was pretty much a nursemaid, I suppose. However, as the family grew and the children got older, I began teaching them to read and write and suchlike until they were big enough to go away to school.'

'You made the move from Wales with this family?'

'That's right, Mr Caunce. Mr Allen is

a master stonemason, you see. He was offered an important position working on the minster, so the family removed to York and took me with them,' she related, adding with a small shrug, 'Their youngest boy is beginning school after Christmas, so there was no longer any place for me with the Allens.'

'I see.'

She'd stopped drinking, and James nudged the tankard back toward her. 'You didn't wish to return to your family in Conwy?'

'They're all gone now, Mr Caunce. My mother died when I was young, and Da passed away almost two years ago.'

'I'm sorry to hear that,' he said, his gaze falling to the remainder of liquid in the tankard. 'I've quite recently lost my own father.'

Meirian murmured her sympathy, however James Caunce raised a hand as though to silence her condolences. 'My father and I were not close, Miss Penlan. Indeed, we'd been estranged these past eight years. It was his death which took me back to Blackthorn. He died very suddenly. I was in Spain and the news was several months reaching me.' His clear blue eyes were suddenly clouded and distant. 'I had to resign my commission and come home. The eldest son, you see.'

'You were in the army, where the fighting is?' she murmured at length. 'My brother Dafydd was in the army. He was lost in battle this spring.'

'Damn shame.' James Caunce drained his tankard, staring into the grey embers of the dying fire. 'I saw too many good men give their lives in the madness of that war. Are you alone in the world?'

'Except for Cousin Hafwen. It's thanks to her I got an introduction to Mrs Caunce,' replied Meirian, adding in her blunt fashion, 'You said we had a long journey to Blackthorn, but if the road is flooded, how will we get there? Indeed, how did *you* get from there to here?'

'Witchcraft!' he returned blithely,

then grimaced and lowered his voice. 'I should be more careful what I say. The landlord likely still believes in the black arts — we're only a crow's flight from the old witches' nest of Pendle, you know! But to answer your question, I came by sculler.' He laughed out loud at Meirian's startled expression. 'You know what one is, then?'

'Of course I do,' she returned. 'Although I've never been in one, nor wanted to either.'

'It's the only way, I'm afraid. The monks of Blackthorn used scullers in the olden times, and we still do for getting around the meres,' he explained. 'They're pretty useful for crossing flooded land, too.'

'Ah, well,' remarked Meirian practically, 'there's a first time for everything.'

'That's the spirit!' He grinned. 'We paddle across the flooded fields and then get onto the river between the hills and away out to Blackthorn. As soon as you've finished your drink, we'll be on our way.'

'I'm ready,' Meirian replied, taking another sip of the potent brew but quite unable to drain the tankard as her companion had done. 'The driver has brought in my box from the coach, and I have a carpetbag.'

'You'll have to leave your box here,' James said, glancing at the locked and bound wooden chest stowed beside the settle. 'I'll charge the landlord to have it brought up to Blackthorn as soon as the water goes down.'

Meirian followed him from the tavern into the winter night. The wind had dropped considerably, but the rain continued to fall straight and heavy as nail-rods. Taking her bag, James Caunce raised a lantern with one hand and grasped Meirian's arm with the other, steadying her when she might have slipped on the muddy, sloping ground.

'The sculler's tied up to the gorse.' He pointed ahead, pushing the carpet-bag at her. 'Take hold of your bag and I'll carry you.'

'There's no need — '

'The water's only calf-deep just here,' he went on, sweeping her up into his arms and splashing into the murky water towards the small boat. 'But it's enough to soak your skirts.'

Meirian felt unsteady in the shallow flat-bottomed sculler, her cold wet hands gripping tightly the two coarse jute loops James Caunce pressed into them.

'Keep as low as you can, Miss Penlan. Whatever you do, don't let go of the ropes,' he instructed. 'It's going to be choppy enough going over the fields, but once we get onto the river the current's rough and fast. If you go over the side there, you'll be swept away.'

He extinguished the lantern and the night plunged into total blackness once more. Meirian caught her breath when the flimsy little boat rocked as James Caunce climbed aboard, gasping as he loosed the mooring rope and suddenly the sculler pitched forward into the swell of the surging floodwater. She could hear the groan and creak of the paddle and had not the slightest notion of how he was locating their direction. The boat bounced and spun, catching branches and bushes, swirling on eddies and crashing against unseen flotsam and jetsam.

Meirian's arms and shoulders ached with the strain of holding fast to the ropes, and her entire body was sore and stiff from the tension of flattening herself against the coarse timbers of the sculler's bottom. She had little idea how much time was passing or how many miles they'd covered when she felt the warmth of James Caunce's breath against her cold cheek.

'We're still over land!' he shouted close to her ear. 'Any minute we'll be swept onto the river, so brace yourself. It's not far now. We're on a straight course to the boathouse.'

Meirian hung on even tighter to the ropes. Suddenly her stomach lurched as the flimsy craft was tossed into the seething turbulence of the swollen river.

The surging current rushed and roared in her ears, great waves of it crashing into the sculler and soaking her clothing, hair and face with ice-cold water.

The deafening cacophony of sound altered, and Meirian heard the scraping of rocks against the hull; felt the closeness of dripping overhanging trees. Even though she could not see anything of her surroundings, she had the sensation of being borne rapidly down an endless claustrophobic tunnel. She was distantly aware of James Caunce's ragged breathing as he fought to maintain a steady course and keep them from being dashed to pieces against the jagged outcrops.

Then it was over. A sudden massive jolt halted the sculler's progress. The river was pounding against the timbers, the craft straining to follow the swift current. Holding on all the tighter to the ropes, Meirian sensed she was alone in the boat and realised James Caunce was ashore, hauling the sculler from the teeming waters up onto dry land. For a moment, she simply lay still, breathless and exhausted.

James lit the lantern, and in its glow Meirian saw that his face was streaked with mud and rain. Where a sharp branch had torn across his cheek, blood oozed from a deep gash. Extending both hands, he helped her to sit. 'Take as much time as you need. We've a short walk through the woods to my bailiff's cottage. I've left horses there. Do you ride?'

'I'm afraid not,' she replied, clambering out to stand beside him on the riverbank.

'No matter. You can ride in front of me,' he replied, dragging the boat all the way up the sloping, muddy ground and into the boathouse. 'Do you need to rest a while?'

Meirian shook her head. Soaked to the skin and dithering with cold, all she wanted was to reach their destination as quickly as possible. 'Let's keep going. I'll warm up once I start walking.'

'It's not very far.' He took the carpetbag and held the lantern higher so it might cast a better beam upon the bridle path winding away through the woods. 'The lanes are far too muddy for even the wagon to travel without getting bogged down, so horseback was the only option.'

The ancient woodland closed around them as they walked, cocooning them from the rush of the river and sheltering them considerably from the worst of the rain. 'There! That light through yonder is from the bailiff's cottage,' James announced at last. 'It's but a short ride from there up to the manor house.'

They approached a small cottage buried deep in the woods. The low square windows showed light, and plumes of smoke rose from the chimney. As they neared the door, Meirian heard the whicker and stamp of horses from the adjoining stone stable. The cottage door was drawn open but a crack in response to James's knock, though it was sufficient for her to glimpse several men gathered about a table bearing ale and playing cards.

Not a one looked from his drinking and gaming as the bulky red-haired bailiff peered around the partially open door. Meirian noticed that James's shrewd gaze was directed beyond the bailiff to the individuals gathered within. The bailiff obviously noticed it too, for he closed the door behind him and stepped out onto the rough cobbles.

'Miss Penlan, this is Tod Weir, Bailiff of Blackthorn.'

'How do you do, Mr Weir,' she responded, taken aback at the suspicion in the narrowed eyes of the stocky middle-aged man. Meirian instantly disliked him.

'Miss Penlan,' Weir said with a nod, brushing by her as he started from the cottage and led the way along to the stables. 'I'm very glad to see you're not afraid of restless spirits. The prospect of living in a house possessed by the dead clearly hasn't put you off joining our close-knit little community — '

'That's enough, Tod!' cut in James, taking Meirian's arm. 'I doubt Miss Penlan gives credence to such jolly robins. We're just taking Swift tonight. Bring Misty back up to the house in the morning.'

'Just as you like, Captain,' returned Weir, opening up the stable doors. 'Swift's all saddled and waiting for you.'

'Is George Legh in the cottage bending his elbow and losing his pay to you and your cronies?' enquired James easily, going to one of the stalls and leading out a tall bay.

'I'm sure I haven't seen him these past few days, Captain Caunce. Our paths have little cause to cross.'

'If you *should* happen across Legh, make sure he gets home to the schoolhouse before he drinks himself senseless,' commented James, setting Meirian securely onto the bay. 'And at first light, ride down along the Bottoms and make sure the flocks are brought up away from the riverbank. Check the woollers' cottages, too. If they look like flooding out, get the tenants to take the fleeces and finished stuff up to the school out of harm's way. It'd be an idea to warn the vicar if the river bursts its banks, as he may have unexpected house guests at St Radegund's. Len's not fond of surprises.'

Tod Weir stood aside at the stable doors as James walked the bay out into the rain. 'Will there be anything else, sir?'

Gathering up the reins, James mounted and glanced down at the bailiff. 'Meet me at the house as soon as you're back from the village tomorrow morning. I intend getting an early start out to the quarry.'

'Just as you want, Captain. Good night, Miss Penlan. My apologies if I alarmed you with tales of hauntings at Blackthorn, for there's surely nothing to it.'

'I'd be astonished if there were,' returned Meirian in her forthright fashion. 'Although your apology is appreciated, it is quite unnecessary. I wasn't in the least alarmed. Good night to you, Mr Weir.'

'Well, that told him,' murmured James close to her ear, as Swift started at a walk away from the bailiff's cottage and along a path weaving deeper into dense woodland. 'You're a woman who speaks her mind, I'll say that for you!'

'My sharp tongue has got me into bother more than once, Mr Caunce,' she admitted, adding curiously, 'What on earth are 'jolly robins'?'

'Daft notions.'

She craned her neck around to look at him. 'I beg your pardon?'

He laughed out loud. 'That wasn't a response to your question, Miss Penlan. It was the answer!'

'I've not heard the expression before.' She smiled, adding soberly, 'Why was that man so disagreeable?'

'Didn't you like my bailiff?'

She turned again, although in the darkness could scarcely see the eyes her gaze met. 'If it's the truth you want, no. No, I did not. I thought he was very unpleasant. What was all that silliness about the house being haunted, anyway?'

Meirian heard James draw in a slow breath before answering. 'I told you my father died last year. Well, he died unexpectedly. Mysteriously, many folk thought. In a secret room under the eaves where a priest was murdered more than two hundred years ago.'

She stared at him with horror. 'Your father wasn't *killed*, was he?'

'No . . . but lots of people hereabouts are still very superstitious,' continued James at length. 'When my father died so suddenly in the priest's room — a room already shrouded in fear and dread because a priest's blood has been shed there . . . Well, talk of evil and hauntings whipped up like wildfire.'

'Because two awful things happened centuries apart in the same room?' she queried incredulously.

'The old ways and beliefs live on in

an isolated place like Blackthorn, Miss Penlan. Folk still bury infants' shoes under their doorsteps.' He continued grimly, 'Our cook swore she saw something not of this world. Edna Thwaite was born and bred in the manor house, but she vowed never to set foot there again as long as she lived. Wouldn't even go back to pack her belongings. Your cousin had to do it for her.'

'I've never heard anything like it.'

He shrugged. 'What Edna said frightened the daylights out of the rest of the servants, and most of 'em left with her. People are too scared to work at the manor house anymore.'

They travelled on in silence, the sodden ground inclining steeply beneath the horse's sure hoofs. Meirian caught herself leaning back heavily against James Caunce's chest as they rode, her eyelids heavy.

'Are we in Blackthorn yet?' she murmured, struggling to keep her tired eyes open.

'Have been since the river. That's the boundary of Blackthorn land,' he answered easily. 'There aren't any bridges nearby, so the only way across is with the ferryman some miles downstream. You can't get your bearings tonight, but roughly speaking, we have the river to our right and Swallowhole Mere away over through the woods to the left. It's some three miles long and is the longest in the whole of Lancashire.'

'Mrs Pickles from the stagecoach mentioned 'meres'. What are they?'

'Lakes. Blackthorn's patchworked with them, but Swallowhole's by far the biggest and deepest. There's an island in the middle that used to be a holy place when monks lived here. They had a hermitage on it. After the monks went, the Caunces added the monastery's land to their own and built a hunting lodge on Hermitage Island,' explained James wryly. 'With the trees being bare, you'll be able to glimpse Swallowhole from the window of your room. The manor house stands between the mere and the river.'

They presently emerged from woodland into a clearing, and James swung down from the saddle before a dimly lit white and brown timber-framed manor house. Taking Meirian in his arms, he lifted her down and held her steady a moment until she gained her footing on the wet cobbles.

'Before I take Swift around to the stables, I'll show you inside.'

He led her up four worn stone steps to a massive and ancient timber door, turning the twisted iron ring and pushing it back against creaking hinges. Candles in glasses burned from sconces along a stone-flagged screened passage, their flickering flame-shadows set leaping by the gust from the open door.

'This is the Great Hall,' said James, his voice and boots echoing eerily upon the stone flags as they went around the huge carved screen into a shadow-filled, barn-like room. 'In medieval times, it would've always been crowded and busy with feasts and manor courts and celebrations. It's rarely used now.'

'It's like being inside a castle!' exclaimed Meirian, when James lit a lantern and she took in the cavernous fireplace and tall arched windows with their vivid stained-glass panels. 'How old *is* this house?'

'Too old,' said James with a grin. Meirian turned her face upward, gazing into the depths of the high vaulted ceiling with its mighty hammer-beams and heavily carved bosses bearing angelic faces and coats of arms.

'There've been Caunces at Blackthorn since the year dot, but this house was built in the 1500s. I don't doubt it was then the height of luxury, but now it's definitely seen better days. My father's wanton neglect of house and estate didn't help any, either.' He set the lantern upon a settle and gestured for Meirian sit. 'I'll fetch Hafwen.'

James's boots rang out on the stone flags as he disappeared beyond the screen, leaving Meirian alone in the

Great Hall of Blackthorn. She rose, wandering the length of it and holding the lantern high to better see. It was a cheerless, empty place with little sign of life or occupation apart from a long table and huge carved mahogany chairs at the far end opposite the screen.

She suddenly froze where she stood; she could hear *murmuring*. Muffled and distorted mutterings. Not from anywhere close by, but somehow from *above* her. The disembodied voices were in the very air of the Great Hall itself! A foolish shiver of fear trickled the length of Meirian's spine, and Tod Weir's words crowded upon her.

The whispers were chasing and echoing around and around the Great Hall high above her head. Convinced there must be *someone*, Meirian jerked the lantern about to discover who was there trying to scare her. Nobody was. She was quite alone.

Spinning on her heel, her boots were clattering loudly across the flags when an unearthly scream rent the musty air.

She cried out as a formless, fluid spectre appeared from the darkness of the vaulted ceiling and came straight at her. Even as Meirian shrank back, she felt the air stirring close to her face, and something gossamer-soft brushed her cheek.

Meirian reeled, the lantern's beam a wild arc as the gleaming white phantom swooped the length of the Great Hall. It wheeled around, soaring back toward her, and she saw the ghostly apparition properly for the first time.

'You're a fine ghost and no mistake!' she muttered, her heart slowing to something approaching normal. 'You certainly scared the daylights out of me.'

Expelling a huge breath and chiding her skittishness, she stood perfectly still and watched as the ghostly pale owl glided gracefully past her to vanish up into the silent recesses of the vaulting once more.

Unexpectedly weak at the knees, Meirian sank onto the settle and held the lantern with both hands. Now that she thought about it rationally, the strange whisperings were easily explained. The wind would whistle and moan through dozens of cracks and crannies in a draughty old place like this. It smelled damp and musty, too.

Presently, brisk footfalls pattered nearer along the passageway, and a plump little woman wearing a crisp white apron appeared from around the carved screen. Meirian was instantly on her feet and rushing to greet her mother's cousin.

'Haffie!'

'It's gradely to see you, pet!' she exclaimed, hugging Meirian tight. 'My, but you've grown!'

'It *is* a long time since we've seen each other,' laughed Meirian. 'I was only twelve.'

'Your mam's funeral,' said Hafwen, nodding sadly. 'I was right sorry to hear about your da. And poor Dafydd too.'

Meirian's eyes clouded. 'I wasn't able to get to Conwy to say goodbye to Da, you know. The Allen children were poorly with scarlet fever and the Mr and Mrs couldn't spare me from York to go home and see him buried. At least I know Da's resting beside Mam at St Agnes. It troubles me, wondering which foreign soil Dafydd lies in.'

'He was a fine young lad and no mistake. He visited me here once when he was on his way to join his regiment. So tall and fine he looked in his uniform.' Hafwen patted Meirian's hand and led her from the Great Hall. 'At least we have each other now, eh? I'm so glad the missus decided to take you on, Meirian. It'll be lovely having you here. Come on, I'll show you your room.'

Extinguishing the lantern and leaving it on the low chest in the screen passage, Meirian followed Hafwen up a short turned staircase carpeted in turkey red and cobalt blue. As they climbed the first flight and reached the turn, the glow from Hafwen's candle flame lighted upon the portrait of a tall elegant woman, illuminating the gleaming amethyst necklace at her throat.

'What a beautiful painting!'

'That's the missus,' said Hafwen fondly, pausing so the candlelight lingered upon the likeness. 'Painted by her son. Not Captain James. The younger one, Lyall.'

'He's certainly a fine artist,' remarked Meirian, who'd frequented the galleries in York on her days off. 'It's so . . . striking.'

'Lyall wasn't much more than a lad when he did that, either,' went on Hafwen, continuing up the stair. 'He's to have his very first exhibition in the New Year. You'll meet him tomorrow.'

Meirian followed her along a wide carpeted passage with small pen-and-ink landscapes and cross-stitched samplers hanging upon the walls.

'Your room is here at the end. It's got fine views across the gardens to Swallowhole Mere,' went on Hafwen, opening a door and touching her flame to the candle standing on a low carved cabinet. 'It's a nice room, but it hasn't been used in a long while, so I've had the fire burning all day and put a warming pan in your bed to make it cosy.'

'It's lovely and homely, Haffie!' Meirian beamed, squeezing her cousin's rough hand and gazing about the airy room with its square leaded window, thick curtains, woven rug and big comfortable bed. 'Thank you for going to such trouble.'

'It's been a pleasure getting it ready for you,' said Hafwen with a smile, closing the curtains and stirring the fire into a blaze. 'Get yourself out of those sodden clothes, and I'll fetch up hot water so you can have a nice wash and get straight into bed.'

'I had to leave my box at the tavern,' began Meirian, drawn to the comfort and warmth of the crackling fire. 'But I've got my carpetbag with my personal things.'

'Just let me know if there's anything else you need to tide you over. After you've bathed, I'll bring you a brew and a bite to eat — there's soup heating on the stove. Then you must get some sleep.' Hafwen bustled across the room, pausing with her hand upon the door to look back at her kinswoman. 'Welcome to Blackthorn, Meirian. I hope you'll be happy here.'

2

Rain was streaming down the small diamond-shaped panes of the window when Meirian stirred a few hours later. The sky was growing light and she turned onto her side, watching the rain and listening to the quietness. At the Allen household, she had been accustomed to awakening to the noise, clamour and smoke of a busy town. Here at Blackthorn, however, there was just the gurgle and gush of water, the ebb and rush of wind surging through bare winter trees, and wavering evergreens.

Shivering, Meirian slipped from beneath the covers and hurriedly washed with cold water from the pitcher. The fire was almost ashes and she dressed quickly in the thick woollen skirt, bodice and shawl Hafwen had put out for her.

Vigorously brushing out her dark brown hair, Meirian moved across to the window and leaned out a little way, breathing in the clean damp air and sharp scent of pines and getting her first proper sight of her new home.

Deftly pushing the last couple of pins into her hair, she wrapped the shawl a little closer and went out along the passage to the stairs, pausing to look again at the portrait of the squire's widow. Even in the dim morning light filtering through the old glass of the tall lancet window, the painting of Isabelle Caunce wearing the plainest of gowns with the exquisitely beautiful amethyst necklace had a luminous, quite startling quality.

Once down the stairs, Meirian hesitated in the carpeted passage beside a loudly ticking clock, unsure which was the way to the kitchen and unwilling to start opening the row of closed doors lest she barge in upon the family at breakfast. She'd gone just a few yards further down the passage when carpet gave way to bare flags and a young woman emerged from around a corner carrying two laden coal scuttles.

'You must be Miss Rees's cousin,' said the girl with a smile. 'I'm Gladys. Are you settling in all right?'

'Yes, thanks. I'm Meirian. Here, let me give you a hand with those.'

'Oh no, miss, you can't,' protested Gladys, but Meirian had already wrested away one of the heavy scuttles.

They continued along the passage and around into an attractive room with a low window overlooking a walled garden. 'This is the drawing-room,' said the maid, hurrying inside and putting the scuttle down on the hearth. 'Thanks for your help, miss. We haven't got many servants here now since Cook saw the ghost, so it'll be nice having somebody young about the place. I'm glad you've come.'

'On the journey yesterday, I wasn't at all sure I was doing the right thing,' confided Meirian frankly. 'But when I woke up this morning, I just felt in my bones this was where I was meant to be.'

'Fate, like!' said Gladys, nodding. 'I know what you mean. I felt that way when I met Alf. He's the stable lad.' She giggled. 'Him and me are meant to be together, only he doesn't know it yet! I'll show you back to the kitchen.'

'There's no need, Gladys,' said Meirian with a smile. 'I can find my way now. See you later.'

Retracing their steps along the passage and following the smell of baking bread, she turned in at an open doorway and found Hafwen alone in the warm low-ceilinged kitchen.

'Hello, Meirian love!' she said, beaming, as she turned around from the pots steaming and bubbling pots on the stove. 'Did you sleep well?'

'I did, thank you,' responded Meirian. 'How can I be useful?'

'You can't,' replied Hafwen, ushering Meirian to the table. 'Sit yourself down and I'll get your breakfast.'

'Haffie, I don't want you waiting on

me! You've more than enough to do already.'

'Don't be daft; it's just keeping house for the missus and the boys now. Nothing fine or fancy,' insisted Hafwen, firmly pushing her cousin down onto one of the benches alongside the oblong scrubbed oak table. 'I'm not one to speak ill of the dead, but life in this house has certainly got a lot easier for all of us since the old squire passed away.'

'I believe most of the servants left after he died.'

'That was Cook's fault, silly woman!' Hafwen shook her head impatiently, setting down a dish of porridge before Meirian with a jug of fresh milk and a pot of honey. 'It was her evening off and she was taking a short cut past the house down to the village to visit her brother. Said an evil spirit come chasing out from the priest's room and followed her into the woods. I told her it must've been the owl, but there was no making her see sense.'

'I'll tell you something that really *was* queer, though,' said Meirian, recalling the unsettling sounds she'd heard the night before. 'And I'm certain it was what disturbed the owl and had him flying about. When I was in the Great Hall, the draughts whistling in sounded just like *whispering*, Haffie! Strange murmuring noises, up high in the air somewhere.'

'It'd be folk in the long gallery passing the squint.' Hafwen nodded, rubbing fat into flour at her end of the kitchen table. 'It overlooks the Great Hall, and when everywhere's quiet, voices carry down in a peculiar way.'

'A squint?' echoed Meirian. 'What's that?'

'A hidden peep-hole. I'll show you it when we're up in the long gallery. In the old days when there were spies and all sorts living here, anybody up there in the squint could see and eavesdrop on whatever was going on down in the Great Hall without being seen themselves,' explained Hafwen, adding

47

disparagingly, 'The Caunces must've been an underhanded lot even then.'

'You don't seem to have much regard for the family,' remarked Meirian, gazing across the kitchen to the heavy rain slithering down the window panes. 'Why have you stayed here all these years?'

'Because of the missus,' she answered at once. 'Oh, don't get me wrong, the boys are grand lads and I'm very fond of them. But that said, they *are* their father's sons.

'The missus and me've known each other all our lives, see,' went on Hafwen after a pause. 'My dad was head gardener at Whitfield Park, Isabelle's family home in Cheshire. I was born on the estate a few years before she was. Isabelle was the only daughter in a family of eleven sons, and when we were little we grew up as close as sisters. Even after I went into proper service at Whitfield, we stayed friendly.'

'I didn't know you were born in Cheshire!'

'Dad left Conwy as a boy looking for work. Eventually he fetched up at Whitfield Park and married my ma. She was an upstairs maid there. Grand place it was, too!' she recalled affectionately. 'The missus's family was proper gentry. Wealthy, too. Much richer than the Caunces.'

'So you came to Blackthorn with Mrs Caunce when she married the squire?'

'Aye, and a black day that turned out to be! He was all smiles and pretty words when he came courting her, but once they were wed, Donald Caunce showed his true colours!' The middle-aged woman's cheeks flamed. 'I don't know how the missus put up with him year after year, Especially after what happened with her amethyst necklace. Isabelle's a fine woman, Meirian, and she deserved better than she got from Donald Caunce.'

'When will I meet her?'

'Later this morning,' replied Hafwen as Meirian took her dishes to the sink. 'I'm right glad you've eaten some of that blessed porridge. I've had it ready for hours, and neither of the boys have shown their face yet.'

'The clever, handsome one is here now!' A tall dark-haired man appeared through the garden door, dripping mud and rainwater over the small square passageway. 'I won't come any further till I've taken off these wet clothes.'

'You'd better not,' retorted the housekeeper brusquely. 'I haven't long scrubbed this floor.'

'You must be Hafwen's cousin.' Divested of his boots and outer garments, he came across the kitchen and extended his hand. 'I'm Lyall Caunce — the spare!'

'The spare?' queried Meirian, looking up into expressive brown eyes and an amiable face that was still somehow youthful and mischievous.

'My elder brother James is the heir, which makes me the spare,' he laughed, glancing hopefully around the kitchen like a hungry hound. 'What's for breakfast, Hafwen?'

'Oysters and champagne, same as always,' she responded, banging a basin of porridge onto the table. 'You look the worse for wear. Another late night?'

'Haven't been to bed at all,' he replied, swirling milk into his porridge. 'Stayed up working on a new painting.'

'You've never spent the night on the island!' Hafwen was horrified. 'And come across Swallowhole in this swell?'

'No choice. I was busy painting yesterday and didn't realise how much the water was rising until it was too late. By then it was pitch dark, so I couldn't risk rowing back and disappearing down the swallow hole — ' He broke off, glancing along the table. 'Do you know about the island in Swallowhole Mere, Meirian?'

'Not really.'

'Oh, it's a wonderful place!' he replied enthusiastically. 'You must come out and explore it when the weather settles down. The monks' old hermitage is pretty much a ruin now of course, and I'm using my father's hunting lodge for a studio. It's incredibly peaceful and inspiring. Whenever I'm on the island, I feel as though I could paint forever.'

'Hafwen showed me your portrait of your mother. It's very powerful,' remarked Meirian, warming to the exuberance of the young artist. 'Was it painted on your island?'

'Yes; on Mother's very last visit there. She hasn't been to Hermitage for years now.' He was momentarily thoughtful, going on, 'The amethysts in Ma's necklace came from the island, you know. The monks discovered them and — '

'Damn and blast the man!' swore James Caunce tersely.

The garden door banged open, slammed shut and he strode into the kitchen, careless of shedding mud and water. Tossing his hat and coat across the dresser, James scraped back a chair and sat down heavily, shoving a hand through his shock of wheat-coloured hair. 'Is there a brew on the go,

Hafwen? Last night, I told Tod Weir to get himself down to the village at first light, have the flocks brought up from the bottoms and sort out the wool cottage tenants in case the river runs over. And what's he done this morning? Nowt!'

'I saw Tod when I was coming over from the island,' remarked Lyall. 'But he wasn't heading for the village.'

'I bet he wasn't. How Pa ever saw fit to give Tod Weir the run of the manor and a home for life, I'll never know.'

'No secret about that,' huffed Hafwen, banging bread hot from the oven out onto the table. 'Services rendered, wun't it?'

'Aye, that's about the size of it,' agreed James grimly. 'When Miss Penlan and I were at Tod's cottage during the night, he was in a hurry to shut the door so we wouldn't see who was inside. I reckon George Legh must've been there with the rest of Weir's gambling cronies. He should be opening up the school shortly, but there

53

was no sign of life down at the schoolhouse, damn him.'

'You shouldn't judge George Legh so harshly,' said Lyall mildly, meeting his elder brother's gaze across the table. 'He's miserable and desperately unhappy. You've only to look at him to see that.'

'Drinking himself soft and losing his money to Tod Weir and his mates won't help him any,' returned James caustically, glancing to Meirian. 'George Legh is our schoolmaster, Miss Penlan. He was a good one, too. Taught Lyall and me both before we went away to school in Lancaster.'

'George's wife left him last year, Meirian,' put in Lyall quietly. 'He's never got over it.'

'Tod Weir still hasn't brought Misty up from his cottage, either,' commented James agitatedly. 'The man gets a roof over his head and a damn good wage and he does nothing to earn either! I'll have to find him and see what the devil he's playing at before I ride up to the quarry.'

'No, you go straight up to the quarry as planned. Tod Weir can wait,' said Lyall, finishing his tea. 'I'll go down to the village, see to the flocks and the wool cottages, and look in on Samson's Mill as well.'

'What about your own work?'

'I could do with a break from painting,' replied Lyall easily. 'And I'll see if I can't track down George Legh. He's probably just sleeping it off somewhere.'

'The man's turned into a soak, that's what!' muttered Hafwen as Lyall rose from the table, with his brother making to do likewise. 'And you can just sit down again, squire James! I'm not wasting time and good food making breakfasts that don't get eaten. I had enough of that with your father!' She pushed the hot food in front of James before turning on her heel and leaving the kitchen. 'I'm going up to see the missus has everything she needs, and I'll expect that plate to be empty when I get back.'

'She's a bit fierce, your cousin,' commented James, glancing at Meirian as he started his breakfast. 'Treats me like I'm still six. Her heart's in the right place though. Blackthorn — and my mother — would be lost without her.'

Hafwen returned to the kitchen just as Meirian was washing the breakfast dishes. 'Master James has gone, has he? I'd heard there was trouble of some sort up at the Ormsley quarry. The foreman there is a drinking crony of Tod Weir's.'

'What did you mean about Weir and services rendered?' asked Meirian, recalling her cousin's earlier comment. 'He seems to be a big man around here, but I didn't like what I saw of him last night at all.'

'Tod Weir's a nasty, sly piece of work,' replied Hafwen in disgust. 'Whatever the old squire wanted, Weir made sure he got. But he's not the sort to do owt for nowt. His palms are always well greased, and you can be sure Tod Weir has his thumb in all sorts of pies around

Blackthorn. Leave that now and get yourself tidied up,' she went on, taking a stack of crockery from Meirian's arms. 'I'm to take you up to meet the missus when she has her morning coffee.'

3

Later that morning, Hafwen and Meirian started from the kitchen up to Isabelle Caunce's little parlour.

'What you need to understand before you talk to the missus is that once you've crossed the river and come into Blackthorn, the Caunces own everything and everyone,' explained Hafwen quietly as they climbed the staircase. 'The Caunces built the church and the school and the cottages and the workshops and the mills. They own the quarries and the marl pits, the inn and the farms, the fishing rights and the market days, and just about all the woods and hills and meres and meadows for as far as the eye can see.'

'Everything's so very different from being at the Allens',' murmured Meirian. 'I don't know what to expect, Haffie. I don't even know what duties

Mrs Caunce has engaged me to do.'

'You'll find out soon enough,' was all Hafwen would say.

After passing the portrait, they followed a carpeted passage into a spacious oblong room. Meirian barely had time to take in the rows of paintings, assortment of musical instruments and well-stocked bookshelves before Hafwen pointed to one of the arched door casings. It appeared exactly the same as the others in the row extending the length of the gallery.

'This is the squint. It overlooks the Great Hall, but you'll need to climb up and lean right inside to see out.'

'And down there is where I was waiting for you last night?' queried Meirian in astonishment, kneeling on the smooth ledge and having to crane her neck to peer from the quatrefoil-shaped opening in the wood panelling. 'Why, I'm up amongst the roof beams here — I could reach out and touch that angel's face.'

'Next time you're in the Great Hall,

look up and try to spot where the squint is,' said Hafwen. 'You'll not find it. It's too well hidden amongst the rest of the paneling.'

Leaving the curious squint and the elegant long gallery behind, it was but round another corner and up a short flight of low stairs before Hafwen tapped upon a door and they entered Isabelle Caunce's bright, cosy parlour.

'My cousin Meirian Penlan, missus,' said Hafwen, withdrawing from the parlour. 'I'll fetch up the coffee, and there's walnut cake to go with it.'

Although she'd seen Lyall's portrait of his mother, Meirian was quite taken aback by the regal ramrod-straight woman with iron-grey hair softly pinned about an angular, rather handsome face. She immediately set aside her writing tablet and rose from a desk cluttered with letters, wafers, tablets and journals.

'How delightful it is to meet you, Miss Penlan! May I call you Meirian? Good!' Isabelle Caunce offered her hand in a warm welcome, gesturing toward a well-upholstered sofa. 'Come, sit beside the fire. You'll join me in coffee and cake, won't you? I always have a touch of brandy in my morning coffee — I find it sets me up for the rest of the day.'

'Coffee and cake sounds very nice, ma'am,' replied Meirian hesitantly, unsure how to respond to the informal manner of her new mistress.

'I was greatly impressed with your letters,' went on Isabelle, lighting some sort of long slim cigar. Meirian could scarcely believe her eyes. She'd never before seen a lady, or any woman, smoking. 'You have a fluency of language and an exceptionally beautiful hand. Where did you learn to read and write?'

'At home, ma'am. From my mother,' replied Meirian proudly. 'She loved reading, you see. Ma used to say books are the quietest and most constant of friends.'

'How very true that is! What a

remarkable woman your mother must be,' exclaimed Isabelle with admiration. 'It's hardly a surprise that you too are a great reader.'

'I don't read grand books, ma'am,' she replied seriously. 'My father was very keen on philosophy and politics, but like I told you in my letter, I prefer reading stories.' Meirian's mind all of a sudden darted back to her drab box-room at the Allens', where the little collection of much-loved books had offered a brief escape from hard work and loneliness. 'I love a really good story, ma'am. Where I can lose myself for a while, you see.'

'Yes, Meirian. Yes, I do see,' replied Isabelle quietly. 'I believe you're a woman after my own heart. Ah, here comes Hafwen with our coffee.'

The housekeeper caught Meirian's eye and gave her an encouraging nod as she served the fragrant beverage and thinly sliced walnut cake. 'Will that be all, missus?'

'Yes, thank you.' Isabelle paused,

pouring a measure of brandy from an ornately engraved silver flask into her coffee cup. 'Has Tod Weir brought Misty back yet?'

'No, the lazy good-for-nothing has not!' returned Hafwen. 'I knew you wouldn't want her left down there with him an hour longer than necessary, so I sent young Alf to fetch her home.'

'Well done, Hafwen. That man is quite insufferable.' Isabelle frowned, adding, 'Has James gone to the quarry? I believe there's trouble of some sort.'

'Aye. The squire took himself off up there earlier on.' She paused at the door. 'Oh, Doctor Poulsom's just sent round a note saying he'll be here this evening for chess whatever the weather.'

'Henry Poulsom is our nearest neighbour and has been a dear friend for many years, Meirian,' explained Isabelle as the door closed quietly behind Hafwen. 'We play chess twice each week, and are in the middle of a particularly challenging game. Henry believes he has the beating of me — but he's much mistaken! Did Hafwen bring you through the long gallery? You must feel free to borrow any of the books, or the music. I've gathered together quite a decent library,' she went on, topping up her coffee and adding another liberal dash of brandy. 'Tell me, Meirian, how much do you know of our situation here at Blackthorn?'

'Only what little I've seen since arriving,' replied Meirian truthfully. 'My cousin and I haven't met for many years, and I regret we corresponded but infrequently.'

'Hafwen's not much for letter-writing, it's true,' agreed Isabelle, offering another slice of walnut cake. 'I was widowed last year. Most medieval manor houses are said to have a ghost or two prowling the passages — headless horsemen, weeping lovelorn ladies, all sorts of fanciful nonsense — but since Donald died in the priest's room, local people really have started believing our house is haunted.'

'Captain Caunce mentioned that the

cook and some of the other servants had, er, left.'

'Not so much left as fled as fast and as far as their legs could carry them — spreading gruesome tales as they went,' Isabelle recalled scathingly. 'In this day and age, you'd expect people to be more enlightened, wouldn't you? Anyhow, that's the reason for our dearth of servants. Folk are scared to come and work at Blackthorn. We have only Hafwen and a handful of stalwarts now.'

'I haven't had much experience cooking, ma'am, but I'm quite competent at all other household chores,' Meirian responded, considering her skills. 'It's true your house is far larger than anywhere I'm used to, but if I'm shown what needs to be done, I'm sure I'll be able to — '

'No, no, Meirian. You misunderstand my reasons for asking you to join us here,' interrupted Isabelle. 'Although I don't doubt Hafwen will appreciate any help you can give her, I have engaged you for quite different duties. I want you to take over my responsibilities at Blackthorn so I might write my novel. Heaven knows I've waited long enough.' She rose, sweeping from the parlour and leaving Meirian with no choice but to follow.

'I'll take you down to the study where the household inventories, ledgers and all the estate papers are kept. You'll soon familiarise yourself with how things are done, so don't be alarmed,' continued Isabelle confidently, pausing in the long gallery to point out volumes of all the great works as well as popular modern novels and plays. There was an extensive collection of music, too. Passing the squint, they left the gallery and went along the passage to the staircase. Meirian's gaze was drawn once more to the painting. Now that she'd met and spoken with its subject, she was even more impressed by Lyall Caunce's portrayal.

'Good, isn't it?' remarked Isabelle. 'James says it captures my stubborn, outspoken and domineering nature exactly. Is that what *you* were thinking?'

Meirian was momentarily speechless until she noticed that Isabelle's dark eyes were twinkling at her. 'I was . . . I was just thinking how lively it was, ma'am.'

'Bravo! The perfect answer,' laughed her mistress as they turned down the staircase. 'I'd never been painted and wasn't keen on the notion; however, I'm glad I did it now, not least because that was the very last occasion I wore the amethysts. I'm not a showy woman, but I do confess I really loved that necklace and was terribly sad when it disappeared from the casket in my bedroom.'

'Disappeared?' Meirian echoed curiously. 'Stolen, you mean?'

'Good heavens, there was no question of the servants taking it! My immediate suspicion was Donald purloining it to pay his tailor or wine bill or impress one of his doxies. Of course he swore he hadn't set eyes upon the necklace since I sat for the painting,' reflected Isabelle sombrely. 'I wanted to believe him, Meirian, I really did . . . But whatever the truth of the matter,' she went on briskly, 'the amethyst necklace vanished into thin air more than eight years ago and has never been seen since.'

'Eight years?' mused Meirian with a frown. 'That time rings a bell — ah, I remember! Captain Caunce said he'd joined the army eight years ago.'

'That's right. James went for a soldier a few months after I lost the necklace; and a short while after that, Rosamund — Doctor Poulsom's daughter — left Blackthorn too. It was a peculiar year, one way and another. There's an intriguing legend surrounding the amethyst necklace and a rather curious prophecy — you must ask James to tell you all about it. He was much taken with the tale as a boy,' she concluded, turning a corner into a cluttered room lined with shelves and glass-fronted cabinets. A large desk piled with papers was set before the wide, low window. 'Every document with any significance to the manor of Blackthorn is kept here in the squire's study.'

Meirian nodded, drawing a slow breath and gazing about her. Although she wasn't yet aware of what exactly her duties were to be, she was convinced this draughty, rambling old place with its secrets and mysterious past was where she wanted to be. Moving to the window, she gazed far across the rain-swept gardens, past the sprawling pines and speckled hollies to the gaunt trees screening Swallowhole Mere. Taking another steadying breath, she looked around to face the squire's widow.

'What is it you wish me to do, ma'am?'

Isabelle gave a small smile and indicated they be seated. 'My husband was a difficult and disagreeable man to live with, Meirian. Oh, I loved him deeply when we married, but then I didn't really know him. One doesn't. He inherited Blackthorn within months of our wedding, but from the outset Donald had no interest and very little inclination for the manor. As the years went by, he cared less and less, and shifted his responsibilities as squire more and more to his bailiff.'

'Tod Weir? I met him last night,' commented Meirian, her lips pursed. 'Albeit briefly.'

'Weir's a parasite. He clung to Donald like a leech, and my husband had not the strength nor the wit to break free. He came to rely utterly upon Tod Weir. While Donald lived, that man controlled Blackthorn in all but name, and continued to do so until James came home from Spain and took up his inheritance,' explained Isabelle unemotionally. 'You'll have frequent occasion to deal with Tod Weir, Meirian. Always take the greatest of care. He's devious, and will make trouble for you if he's permitted.'

'I'll be sure to watch my step,

ma'am,' she replied with conviction. 'Although now Captain Caunce is in charge, why doesn't he dismiss Weir and send him away?'

'Donald's Will provided that Tod's position as bailiff be secure and the cottage on the estate remain his in perpetuity.'

'No!' Meirian's jaw dropped in amazement. 'Whyever would the old squire have done such a thing?'

'You might well ask,' replied Isabelle bitterly. 'Frankly, I dread to imagine what the answer might be.'

She opened one of the glass-fronted cabinets. Its shelves were crammed with thick bound ledgers, each spine bearing the period of years the volume covered. 'These are the household ledgers, traditionally kept by the squire's wife. They reach back generations, as you can see. The more you read, the better you appreciate that without the women always holding this estate together, Blackthorn would've fallen to rack and ruin a dozen times over. The squires' wives brought dowries of course, but it's because of their strength, integrity and honesty that Blackthorn survives.' Isabelle paused, running her fingers across one of the worn cloth bindings. 'I love my sons very much, Meirian, but the Caunce male line is weak by nature. Spendthrifts, dilettantes and rogues to a man. My sons have inherited bad blood, and I fear for them. For their well-being, and for their future at Blackthorn.'

Despite the warmth radiating from the crackling fire, Meirian suddenly felt chilled. 'Are these the volumes you've done, ma'am?' she enquired at length, opening one of the thick books. 'Why, it's exactly like a diary!'

'These ledgers chronicle the day-to-day passing of my life since the day I arrived here as a bride. So many years,' reflected the older woman soberly. 'I prided myself upon keeping meticulous records, and while my husband shamefully neglected his duties as squire, I've always taken my responsibilities as the squire's lady very seriously indeed. The servants, tenants and estate workers will be in your care, Meirian. You'll nurse them when they're ill, feed them when harvests are poor, listen to their problems, and take up their grievances to the bailiff,' explained Isabelle quietly, sitting straight-backed beside the desk, her hands folded loosely in her lap. 'The women will especially depend upon you. They come for medicines, advice and sometimes confessions. It must all seem terribly feudal and old-fashioned to a young woman accustomed to the society of a sophisticated town like York, but times don't change in a small country place like Blackthorn.'

'I don't have any experience or qualifications for the work you've described, ma'am,' said Meirian bluntly. 'However, I do want this position very much. I'll work hard and not let you down, but I can't say I'm not daunted by the prospect of such responsibility.'

'Of course you're daunted! And you'll make hideous mistakes — we all have. But you'll do more good than harm, Meirian,' she said firmly. 'I'm an excellent judge of character, and your letters told me a great deal. Blackthorn has been my occupation since I married, I wouldn't be entrusting it into your hands if I were not convinced of your trustworthiness and capabilities.'

Meirian sat staring into the glowing, shifting coals while the clock on the mantel noisily ticked away the minutes. At length, she raised her chin and met Isabelle Caunce's eyes steadily. 'I want to learn as much as I can about the manor house, the village, the tenants and all that goes on at Blackthorn before I actually start doing anything. I'm anxious not to go blundering in to situations I understand nothing about.'

'Begin with the ledgers.' advised Isabelle. 'They give chapter and verse upon household inventories, ordering in of provisions, stores of herbals and remedies, hirings and dismissals, disputes and grievances as well as all the village, school and church calendars at which the squire's lady is expected to preside or attend.'

'Very well, ma'am,' replied Meirian absently, leafing through the first of Isabelle's ledgers. 'Would I be in the way if I stayed here in the study?'

'Not at all. There are maps and drawings of the house and the whole manor over there in that cupboard. It's such a comfortable room, too. I can recommend the winged chair by the window; there's a very pleasant view of the garden from there. I'm having supper with Doctor Poulsom before our chess game, so I won't see you this evening. Come to my parlour in the morning after breakfast, and we'll talk further then.'

'I'm sure I'll have plenty of questions, ma'am.'

'That's only to be expected, Meirian. It's a huge undertaking, but you'll meet the task splendidly,' reassured Isabelle, her step light as though a great burden were lifting from her shoulders. She paused, her hand upon the study door, and glanced back to where the younger woman was already seated at the great desk.

'I really am most grateful to you, Meirian,' she murmured sincerely. 'I've spent the best years of my life fulfilling my duties as the squire's wife, and I don't intend spending whatever's left of it being the old squire's widow.'

★ ★ ★

Meirian curled up into the winged chair with the ledgers stacked on the little rosewood table beside it and set to reading. At first she studied every entry carefully, but as the hours slid away she began to merely glance through page after page of Isabelle Caunce's spidery and not always entirely legible handwriting.

She didn't see Isabelle again, and

both Caunce brothers were out all day. After being accustomed to the clamour of the Allens' crowded household and the constant demands upon her from Mrs Allen and the children, Meirian found Blackthorn blissfully quiet and peaceful, relishing the chance to get on with her work undisturbed.

The afternoon was already closing in to darkness when Hafwen came in with tea. 'Thought I'd bring you a brew to keep your strength up.' She smiled, crossing the study to draw the heavy curtains closed and add more coals to the fire. 'You look like you've been busy!'

'There's an awful lot to take in, Haffie,' confided Meirian, her gaze upon the heap of scattered ledgers and hastily written notes she'd made on a blank tablet. 'I just hope I'm able to perform the duties well enough.'

'You're bright and clever and a hard worker,' said Hafwen, perching on the arm of the couch across the fire from her cousin. 'You'll manage grand!'

'Will I?' she queried softly, sipping the hot tea. 'I had no idea a squire's lady was busy with so many things. As well as running the household, keeping detailed records of all goods and events, tending the sick and helping the poor, people come to her for advice on all sorts. I've lost count of the girls who've wanted love potions, the young wives needing elixirs to become with child, and the farmers asking Mrs Caunce to find them a good, stout wife.'

Hafwen nodded sagely. 'Folk hereabout may look to the squire for their roof and their bread, but it's the missus they depend on for help when they're sick or have troubles.'

Meirian stared at her cousin, apprehension welling within her. 'Haffie, what am I getting myself into?'

'You'll not let anybody down, pet,' said Hafwen, getting stiffly to her feet. 'Put your books aside for a bit and come help me peel tatties for supper. We'll have the boys home before we know it.'

* * *

With the evening meal roasting and simmering on the stove, Meirian returned to the study. She was seated at the big desk, sorting through a bundle of rolled and tied maps and drawings in search of one showing a plan of the village, when the study door swung open on well-oiled hinges.

'My apologies, Miss Penlan.' James Caunce stopped in his tracks, wet, grimy and travel-stained. 'I didn't realise you were working in here.'

'I'll just tidy up,' she began at once, hurriedly re-rolling the drawing she'd spread across the desk. 'I'll take these up to my room.'

'There's no need,' he insisted, crossing to the desk and bending to withdraw a bundle of documents from the top left-hand drawer. 'You were here first. Besides, I've to go down to The Swan after supper. I'm meeting Simon Coates about these contracts. How are you getting on?'

'Honestly?' She grimaced.

'Honestly.'

'My head's whirling like a dervish!' She smiled ruefully up at him as James stood at the corner of the desk. 'Earlier, I believed I was really getting the hang of it all — but now, I can't seem to remember a thing I've read and I can't make sense of what's right before my eyes!'

'Sounds like it's high time you called it a day, Miss Penlan.' He grinned, glancing at his pocket watch. 'It called *itself* a day hours ago.'

She shook her head. 'I need to do a few more things. I'm meeting Mrs Caunce after breakfast tomorrow, you see. I want to be properly prepared.'

He nodded, leaning across the desk to examine the drawing. 'Are you looking for anything in particular?'

'I want to get a clear picture in my mind of what the village looks like, and who and what is where,' she explained, pointing to the elongated sketch before her. 'This one shows the manor house and a church, and that bit has 'village' written on it, but there're no details of houses or farms, or where the doctor lives — and Mrs Caunce said Dr Poulsom's your nearest neighbour. Also, earlier today you spoke of woollers' cottages along the riverbank. I can't find *them* at all.'

'It's a poor drawing. Old, too,' he commented, moving across the room to the corner cupboard. 'The position of places isn't accurate, and there was no attention to scale in those days. The village cross is twice the size of the manor house, and Swallowhole Mere looks like an accidental ink blot! Here, try this one.' While Meirian rolled up the dog-eared sketch, James spread a huge chart across the desk and weighted it down with a couple of seals and the ink well. 'Grandmother Caunce commissioned this from a proper firm in Lancaster soon after my father inherited the manor. It's clear she had far more interest in Blackthorn than he ever did,' commented James caustically.

'There haven't been any significant changes since this was drawn, so it's pretty accurate.'

'There's Hermitage Island!' Meirian exclaimed, pointing to the neatly sketched craggy island in a vast expanse of water that curved like protecting arms around the high land where the manor house stood. 'I wondered where exactly it was. Your brother was telling me about it this morning, and how you spent lots of time there as children.'

'We did. Lyall, Rosamund — Henry Poulsom's daughter — and I practically lived on Hermitage Island in those days, usually seeking treasure. Have you seen Lyall today, by the way?'

Meirian shook her head, already becoming engrossed with the chart mapping Caunce lands and properties. 'However, Haffie told me Mr Lyall has been back from the village. Apparently, George Legh was at the school as usual, the flocks have been brought up from the riverbank, and the tenants have moved the wool up out of harm's way and taken all the finished stuff to the church for safekeeping in case the river floods, although it's not showing any signs of overflowing yet. Then Mr Lyall gathered together his painting things and went across to Hermitage — ' She broke off, glancing from the chart to find James Caunce staring down at her, a broad grin spreading across his face. 'What's so funny? You asked a question, and I answered it!'

'Can't argue with you there.' His grin widened, but the piercing blue eyes were amiable. 'I meant no offence, Miss Penlan. I'm just astounded you've been here less than a day and already know everything that's going on.'

'You're not suggesting I'm a nosey parker, by any chance?' she challenged, holding his gaze. 'I'm merely interested in people and their activities.'

'You'll be in your element around here then,' returned James. 'You could write a book about what folk here get up to.'

'I believe your mother is about to do

so. Well, she's writing a novel at any rate.'

'Oh, Ma's told you about her novel?' He paused at the rumbling echo of the great oak door opening and closing. 'That must be Lyall home from Hermitage. I'm glad he's not intending to spend another night over there.' James glanced to the clock above the mantelshelf. 'I'd best go up and change. I'll see you at supper, Miss Penlan.'

'I — I — ' she faltered. At the Allens', Meirian had never been allowed to dine with the family, and certainly did not expect to do so here at Blackthorn. She could only imagine James had spoken without thought. 'I'd actually like to finish studying these maps, Captain Caunce.'

'You can study them to your heart's content after we've eaten.' He glanced across at her keenly. 'Dining-room's along the passage and around the stairs. I'll give you a shout when supper's ready.'

The dining-room was comfortable and homely, not at all grand and imposing as Meirian had anticipated. There were just James Caunce, Lyall and herself gathered around the table for Hafwen's plain, wholesome cooking. Although Meirian had declined the offer of wine, as she ate she became aware of how very sleepy she was suddenly becoming. Glancing at her companions, she realised it had been a very long and demanding day for them all.

Both men were obviously weary, however Lyall looked utterly exhausted. His naturally rounded face was gaunt and the soft brown eyes encircled with deep smudges of shadow. Even as Meirian's gaze lingered upon Lyall's drawn features, she realised James was watching her observing his younger brother.

'You're not going over to Hermitage again tonight, are you?' he asked, refilling his glass with the rich, rough country wine.

'The water's gone down a fair bit and the mere's calm enough, so I could go back. *Should*, probably. I've certainly got plenty of work to do, but . . . ' Lyall shrugged despondently. 'I've spent hours upon hours trying to get the flesh tones of one of the characters in my harvest picture, and I'm no nearer now than when I started! If anything, it's getting worse instead of better. I feel like scraping the whole thing off and starting again.' He finished morosely, 'Even if I *did* return to Hermitage tonight, I wouldn't paint anything worthwhile.'

'You're pushing yourself too hard,' remarked James. 'You need to get some rest, man. You look terrible.'

'Thanks, that's cheered me up a lot,' returned Lyall. 'I'm tired enough to sleep standing up, so maybe I'll chance having an early night. You should do the same, Meirian — you must be worn out.'

'I *have* felt perkier,' she conceded with a smile. 'I've a fair bit more reading to do first, though.'

'Let me know if you need anything. It takes a while to find your way around all the stuff in that study,' put in James, flexing his shoulders stiffly. 'Ah, I could do without riding down to The Swan tonight, but I need to get some straight answers from Simon Coates.'

'Any idea what exactly is going on at the quarry?' enquired Lyall.

'No.' James exhaled heavily. 'It's a right tangle, but I'll wager Tod Weir is at back of it, lining his pockets.'

They conversed a little while longer, about everything and nothing in particular, and were finishing off Haffie's rhubarb cobbler when Lyall smiled across at Meirian.

'I haven't enquired after your first day at Blackthorn. How are you settling in?'

'Very well, thank you,' replied Meirian warmly, for she'd taken a liking to the quiet-spoken young man from the first moment they'd met that morning. 'Everyone's been so helpful, and the work is going to be really interesting. Oh, that reminds me! Mrs Caunce said I was to ask about the amethyst necklace and a prophecy?'

'That's James's territory. He knows everything about the whole story,' replied Lyall, his smile fading as he drained his wine. 'If you'll excuse me, I'm for my bed. Good night, Meirian. Hope you get somewhere with Simon Coates, James.'

'I'll drink to that!' He raised his own glass as Lyall quit the room, leaning back from the table and considering Meirian a moment before beginning the old family tale. 'Do you know anything about the monasteries and how they came to be closed down?'

'A little. When I was a child in Wales, we visited the ruins of a monastery not far from Shrewsbury. My mother was very interested in history and faith. I remember her telling Dafydd and me the religious houses were great centres of learning and wealth.'

'She was absolutely right. There've been monks in Blackthorn for more than a thousand years, but it wasn't until the Cistercians settled here and built their monastery and the hermitage that one of the brethren found amethyst on the island.'

'Can that really be true?' she asked, her eyes widening. 'That a monk just found them?'

'Amethyst isn't common, but it's not unknown. There are pockets of quartz around the whole county. That said, the three of us spent our entire childhood searching for treasure of any description whatsoever and found nothing but a few old pots and some buckles.' He grinned wryly. 'Anyhow, the Cistercians were incredibly rich and employed the finest craftsmen. The monks had the raw stone cut into gems and set into a solid gold jewel-encrusted cross for their altar.'

'And they had the necklace made too?'

'Not exactly . . . When Henry VIII closed the monasteries, the Caunces lost no time plundering monastic treasuries. They seized the cross, prised out the gems, and had them fashioned into a necklace as a marriage gift for the squire's betrothed. Ever since then, the amethyst necklace has been passed down from bride to bride, until my mother was given it upon her wedding day.'

'There's a prophecy bound up with the necklace?'

'More a curse than a prophecy — probably cast by a disgruntled old monk,' returned James, a touch humourlessly. 'If ever the Caunces lose the amethyst necklace, they'll lose Blackthorn too.'

'But the necklace *is* lost.'

'And the manor house is practically falling down around our ears,' observed James, his eyes downcast as he studied the ruby-red wine swirling around at the bottom of his glass. 'As for the estate, it's riddled with corruption and infested by men fiddling the books and taking backhanders. This prophecy may well be one Lancashire superstition that proves true, Miss Penlan. My father allowed Blackthorn to slide so close to the edge, I'm not sure there's any pulling it back.'

* * *

It was very late and Meirian was in the study, hardly able to keep her eyes open as she pored over one of Isabelle's most recent ledger entries concerning a tenancy disagreement. She had a horrible feeling she'd have to confront Tod Weir about the sheer injustice of it.

'Meirian!'

She hadn't been aware of the door opening, and her chin jerked up to see Lyall Caunce wearing his nightclothes and hovering uncertainly by the doorway.

'I — I'm so sorry,' he stammered. His face was drained of colour, and the hand that gripped the door's edge trembled violently. 'I had no idea you

. . . When I saw the light, I thought James was back, and — '

'Here, come and sit down before you fall down.' Meirian was already at his side, shepherding him toward the couch nearest the fireplace. Her hand briefly brushed his. It was ice-cold and bloodless, yet Lyall's brow and temples were beaded with sweat. She raked the fire so it blazed and crackled. 'Get yourself warmed up. I'll fetch a hot drink.'

'No, really! I mean, it's very kind of you,' he began, raising dark eyes that were far too wide and bright. 'You're working. I don't want to disturb you.'

'You're not, Lyall. I was about to make some chocolate for myself anyhow,' she fibbed, drawing the woollen blanket from the couch and draping it about his narrow shoulders. 'You stay put, and I'll be back in two ticks.'

When Meirian returned with two mugs and a jug of steaming chocolate, she found Lyall Caunce at the fireside where she'd left him, his elbows propped upon his knees and his head bowed into his hands.

'Drink this. It'll make you feel better.' She offered a mug and sat beside him. 'I talk a lot, Lyall. *Too* much, folk often say! But I'm a good listener, too.'

His gaze slid sidelong. After a moment, he expelled a heavy breath and slumped back into the couch's faded upholstery. 'I really am terribly sorry, Meirian,' he murmured after another long pause. 'I can't imagine what you must think of me. It's just . . . I — I haven't been sleeping very well lately.'

'This must be a very anxious time for you,' she said gently, sipping her chocolate. 'What with all the work and preparations for your exhibition, it's not surprising you can't get a decent night's rest. It must be quite a worry.'

'No. No, it isn't anything like that,' he insisted in a small voice, unable to meet her eyes. 'I have . . . dreams. Tonight they were particularly . . . When I woke up, well, I thought James might be home from The Swan, you see. He — he knows. About the dreams.'

'Nightmares, you mean?' she ventured kindly. Lyall was about her own age, yet sitting there hunched and miserable beside her, he looked much younger than she and so very vulnerable. 'Talking about whatever's troubling you really *does* help. I don't know when Captain Caunce will be back from The Swan, but if you like, you can talk to me.'

He darted a glance of sheer desperation toward her before dropping his gaze once more to his clenched hands, the knuckles white and the long fingers knotting and unknotting constantly.

'I didn't have any dreams when my father first died, you know,' he began at last. 'It's only recently. Since the anniversary of his death. They're awful. Terrifying. Always about the priest's room.'

Meirian swallowed hard, gently covering his cold hands with her own warm ones. 'The room where your father died?'

'It's a ghastly place. Black and confined, like a cell. The only light and air comes through a tiny hole right under the roof.' His voice was barely audible. 'That room was built to keep the family priest hidden from the king's commissioners. In Tudor times, the Caunces were recusants.'

'Does that mean they kept the old religion after it was against the law?'

'Yes. The priest was eventually discovered — betrayed by an informant for half a guinea. He was brutally murdered in the hidden room,' mumbled Lyall. 'There were all sorts of rumours . . . Folk swore the priest's blood wouldn't be washed away. No matter how many times the floorboards were scrubbed clean, the next day the floor would be running with blood again.'

'What an appalling story!' she exclaimed, adding before she thought to bite her tongue, 'But it *is* only a nasty story. You surely can't believe — '

'No. No, but . . . ' He shook his head, raising distraught eyes to hers. 'I found my father's body, Meirian. That hidden room's never been used since the day the priest was murdered. It's been shut up all these years. We've no idea why Pa was in there. Never will know now. But it was *I* who went up there and found him!'

'Lyall . . . I'm so very, very sorry,' was all she could say.

'When I have the dreams, I see Pa. In that room.' He slumped forward, his head bowed and his breathing ragged, his whole body racked with dry, painful sobs. 'In the dreams, there's blood everywhere, Meirian, but there *wasn't* any! There wasn't! Not a drop! I *know*, because I *found* Pa!'

Instinctively, Meirian folded her arms about Lyall's shoulders, comforting him as she might a small child. 'Grief is a queer emotion. It's no wonder you're having nightmares. It's always a shock when you lose somebody you love, even when you know the end is near. But with your da . . . Well, the shock was all the greater. His illness striking so suddenly like it did.'

'You don't understand, Meirian. No.' He shook his head vehemently. 'That's what we told everyone. Doctor Poulsom covered it up. Said Pa died from a heart complaint to spare Ma and protect the family from scandal. But it wasn't true!'

Meirian stared at him, suddenly fearful of what Lyall was about to confide.

'Pa didn't die from any illness. He was in fine health and full of life. Yet that day, he took a rope up into the priest's room and killed himself!' Lyall turned tormented eyes to her. 'I'm afraid to sleep in case the dreams come. I feel as though I'm losing my mind. Whatever am I to do?'

★　★　★

As she dressed and made ready for her interview the following morning, Meirian's thoughts dwelled upon Lyall Caunce. Before finally returning to his room last night, he'd sworn her to silence.

'I've told only you and James about the dreams. Nobody else. I couldn't bear it for Ma to find out. She's been through enough.'

'I'll never breathe a word,' Meirian had promised when they'd parted on the landing and retired to their rooms.

Now, standing before the glass as the grey light of another rain-soaked morning crept through her window, Meirian's sombre reflection stared back at her. Heartsore for the sensitive young man who'd trusted her so completely, she well understood his anguish and suffering. For hadn't she had her share of horrific nightmares when news came that Dafydd had been cut down on some distant foreign field?

Taking a steadying breath, she checked her appearance, gave her hair a firm pat into place and left her room, starting briskly along the passage toward Isabelle Caunce's parlour.

'You'll do splendidly, my dear! Splendidly!' enthused Isabelle after Meirian had asked many questions and their lengthy discussions upon her new responsibilities were drawing to a close. 'While Donald was alive, I fulfilled my duties as the squire's lady. Most people expect me to continue doing so until James takes a bride, but frankly, enough is enough. You can't imagine how glad I am to have found you, Meirian,' she continued blithely. 'Your being here will afford me the liberty to achieve my dearest wish.'

'Writing a novel,' mused Meirian in wonder. 'It's going to be so exciting, ma'am!'

'I've longed to do it since I was a girl. I adore literature and art.' She beamed, pouring more coffee. 'It's from my family Lyall inherits his love of painting, you know. Traditionally, the Caunces are absolute barbarians. If they can't drink it, hunt it or make love to it, they simply aren't interested. It was in the latter circumstances, of course, that the amethyst necklace came into being. Did you ask James about the prophecy?'

'I did. He told me all about it, and how the amethysts were stolen from the monks' cross to make the necklace.'

'So the squire might seduce the heiress he was courting. To marry a wealthy woman is the ambition of all Caunce men, Meirian — that, and the pursuit of the many and varied pleasures life offers a gentleman of leisure,' she went on airily, adding brandy to her coffee. 'Oh, they're devilishly handsome and charming. Any one of them can sweep a girl off her feet without even trying. But unfortunately they're also consummate liars and deceivers who are greedy, unscrupulous and utterly, utterly faithless.'

Although Meirian was quickly becoming accustomed to Isabelle's disarmingly frank outlook, she couldn't help but interject. 'I don't doubt that was the case in the past, ma'am. However, I've found Captain Caunce and Mr Lyall to be very fine young men indeed,' she said, realising too late she should perhaps keep her opinions to herself. 'That is to say, I've only been here a short while and am a total stranger to them both, yet I've never in my life met two gentlemen more courteous, kind and willing to help.'

'Ah, there you have it! Appearances can be treacherous, Meirian.' Isabelle waved a dismissive hand. 'Take Donald — the most noble, handsome and beguiling of men. Yet in truth, he was the most appalling example to his sons. Until the day Donald died, I fought tooth and nail against his pernicious influence upon their hearts and minds. The worst of it was the fact that they were devoted to him, especially as boys. They worshipped the ground he walked on,' she continued sadly. 'They were just children, of course. They couldn't see beyond the smiles, presents and empty promises.'

Meirian drew breath to comment, recalling James's obvious animosity toward his late father, but upon this occasion succeeded in holding her tongue.

'I did my best to bring them up to be honest and trustworthy. And my sons are without doubt the best of the Caunce line,' reflected Isabelle, moving across the parlour to stare from the rain-washed window out across the wet wintry gardens. 'Nonetheless, I don't envy their brides. James and Lyall are good men, but there's an old saying that bad blood will out.' Isabelle turned, silhouetted against the grey light from the window, meeting the younger woman's gaze sombrely. 'And they both have the Caunce hot blood racing in their veins, Meirian.'

4

During those first weeks at Blackthorn, Meirian became more and more convinced Isabelle Caunce's doomladen view of her sons' character was completely wrong. As she settled into her duties at the manor house and around the village, Meirian continued to find both James and Lyall kind, friendly, and ever willing to help. She was thoroughly enjoying her new post and already loved the ancient house with its draughts and creaking timbers. For the first time in many years, Meirian was beginning to feel a real sense of belonging, and part of a family again. With Christmas only a month away, she was happily anticipating the festive season, and every spare moment was spent in the kitchen helping Hafwen with the Yuletide baking, preserving, pickling, and pudding-making.

'Haffie reckons we're weeks behind her usual routine for Christmas cooking,' Meirian was saying, her pen poised above a letter, after Isabelle Caunce had wandered into the study with a tray of coffee. It was still early and not light yet, but the whole household had been up and about for hours. 'We'll get everything done in time, though.'

'Oh yes, I'm sure you will. The pair of you are working wonders, Meirian. Wonders!' remarked Isabelle with a contented sigh, sipping the fragrant brandy-laced coffee. 'The most marvellous Christmassy aromas of oranges, spices, honey and dried fruits are emanating from the kitchen at all hours of the day and night. I'm afraid Christmas at Blackthorn hasn't been a very festive occasion of late,' she went on reflectively. 'However this year we'll dispel all the shadows, make merry and bring the old house back to life.'

'You're really very fond of the manor house, aren't you?' said Meirian with a smile, glancing across the hearth to her mistress.

'I adore every stick and stone of the place,' admitted Isabelle, her dark eyes shining. 'Despite Blackthorn's isolation and being regarded by outsiders as barely civilised, I have many dear friends here and wouldn't dream of living anywhere else. Mind you, I *am* relieved you're distributing the Feast Day tharcakes this year — I'm hoping to make inroads into my next chapter today.'

'Until I helped Haffie make them, I hadn't any notion what a tharcake was,' confessed Meirian wryly. 'I'm still not certain what I'm to do with them once I get them down to the village.'

'Well, the very first thing is to take a parcel of them down to Becky Beswick's cottage. Have you met Becky yet? Not to worry, James will introduce you. Always keep a special eye on Becky for me, Meirian. Beneath that cur-mudgeonly exterior, he's a kind-hearted soul and as honest as the day as long

— which doesn't always gain him friends in Blackthorn.'

'Isn't he the very old man with the peg leg?' queried Meirian, recalling a bent figure as thin as a dry twig and every bit as weathered. 'Apart from bidding him good day, I've never spoken to him, but I've seen him about gathering kindling and hedging.'

'Becky can turn his hand to just about any task — he's had little choice to do otherwise since being invalided out from the navy. He's quite alone in the world, keeps himself to himself, and is far too proud to accept baskets from the 'big house'. However, Becky is especially partial to Feast Day tharcakes, so he gets a special share all to himself. Whenever he's up here working around the garden or house, be sure to tell Hafwen, so she can make sure he doesn't go home hungry.'

'I'll be sure to always look out for him, ma'am,' promised Meirian. 'And I'll ask James to take me to Mr Beswick's cottage as soon as we get to the village.'

'Oh, James and Becky are old friends. Becky taught the boys everything about the woods and the animals and the seasons,' went on Isabelle thoughtfully. 'As for the rest of the Feast Day celebrations, it's all quite straightforward really. The schoolchildren adore it, of course. Anything involving food and a half-day holiday is splendid with them, so you'll get a fine welcome at the school. Reverend Sutcliffe's sermon is usually mercifully brief. After that, the church bell rings, and St Radegund's Feast Day Fair is declared well and truly open.'

'Yesterday afternoon when I was taking the post down to The Swan, there was already a great stream of strangers, fancy floats and carts piled high with tents and goods of every description,' said Meirian. 'When Gladys told me the fair was a grand affair, I didn't imagine it would be so huge or bring so many people from outside.'

'Mmm, there'll be scores more by

today,' replied Isabelle matter-of-factly. 'St Radegund's Fair is the biggest day of the year, but there isn't anything to be apprehensive about. Besides, James will be at your side. He's the squire, so it's his show really. The lady simply smiles a great deal and distributes the tharcakes to our neighbours,' concluded Isabelle. 'My new chapter awaits! Oh, I'm having supper at Henry's this evening. It's our chess night. The poor man's convinced he's devised a new strategy for besting me . . . '

* * *

Replacing a book she'd borrowed upon the shelves of the Long Gallery, Meirian paused and gazed up into the face of the late squire. The portrait hung above the fireplace next to the alcove and showed Donald Caunce in the prime of life. He stared imperiously down from the canvas, gun dogs at his feet and a brace of richly plumed waterfowl across his arm. He'd been a handsome man, certainly. The very first time Meirian had noticed the painting, she'd assumed it to be of James. Both men had the same clear, startlingly blue eyes and shock of wheat-coloured hair. However, upon closer inspection, Meirian realised the father had a certain slackness of jaw, a weakness about the full mouth and an indolence to his arrogant gaze which his eldest son had not inherited.

Turning away from the likeness, Meirian drew her shawl closer and went briskly along the gallery, not sparing a thought to the hidden peep-hole as she passed it by. Running an eye over the neatly written list of chores needing to be done that day, Meirian hurried down the turned stair and along to the kitchen. Isabelle was right — it *did* smell very Christmassy, with the heady aromas of mulling, baking and pickling. The low-ceilinged room was filled with steam as puddings simmered, and Hafwen was lifting yet another batch of coarse oat rounds from the hearthstone when Meirian went in, already tying on her apron and rolling up her sleeves to lend a hand with that day's vegetable peeling.

'I've just had young Alf poking his nose around the garden door in the hopes of catching little Gladys here on her own,' remarked Hafwen, chipping sugar from the loaf and scooping it into the grinder. 'His face dropped longer than a week's wet washing when the poor lad saw me instead! Anyhow, he was saying the river's gone down considerably, so there'll be a lot more folk able to come over for the fair.'

'Are you going?' asked Meirian, getting started on the potatoes. 'Gladys was telling me there'll be fire-eaters and fortune-tellers and all manner of curiosities.'

'St Radegund's Fair is the grandest in the whole county, some say,' remarked Hafwen, adding grimly, 'Merchants and traders come from all over, and so do plenty of charlatans, rogues and pickpockets, so you mind how you go.'

'I'm hoping to have a really good look around.' Meirian was gradually squirreling away festive little gifts for her cousin and new friends. 'Although I doubt I'll have the time. James told me about the river going down when he came into the study earlier this morning. My box will be coming over from Butcher's tavern, and James said after the ceremonies in the village, we'll drive out to the crossing and collect it. He reckons this is a good opportunity for me to meet the ferryman and his family, as well as the other tenants who live in that part of the manor.'

'I'd have thought most of them'd be at the fair,' commented Hafwen, milling the sugar and not looking up at the younger woman. 'Don't get me wrong, Meirian. I'm right pleased you're getting along so well with the family — especially Captain James, for he's the one you've mostly to work with — but you will take care, won't you?'

'About what, exactly?' replied Meirian briskly, busy with her peeling.

'The squire,' answered Hafwen uncomfortably. 'True enough, since he came back to Blackthorn, James hasn't done much in the way of gallivanting. Mind, he's been so busy he's likely not had enough time to catch breath yet. But when he was younger, before he upped and left suddenly like he did, well . . . James had quite a reputation, Meirian,' she continued quietly, meeting her cousin's gaze across the scrubbed table. '*Like father, like son* was said about him more than once. Then there were rumours after he went away. So don't go doing anything daft, pet! Don't lose your head or your heart, for no good'll come from it.'

'Oh for goodness sake, Haffie,' responded Meirian impatiently, tumbling potatoes into a pot and turning to the range. 'I know you mean well, but James Caunce is my employer — or rather, his mother is — and I would no more allow myself to become . . . *fond* . . . of him than I would've to Mr Allen in York.'

'There're big differences between the two,' persisted Hafwen stoically. 'Mr Allen was a much older man, and married with a growing family. The young squire is none of them.'

'Haffie, once and for all — '

Meirian spun around from the range, hands planted firmly on her hips and her cheeks flushed from the fire, but before she could finish, the garden door burst open and with a couple of lithe strides, Lyall bounded into the kitchen and broke the tension.

'Finished my harvest picture at last!' he announced, his smile growing even wider as he slipped around Meirian's side to steal a warm tharcake from the oblong willow basket on the dresser. 'These look good — did you make them?'

'Haffie and I did them together.' She slapped his hand as he made to reach for another of the crumbly oat cakes. 'They're for the village folk after church!'

'I don't go to church,' protested

Lyall, his eyes dancing. 'Surely that means I can eat mine now.'

'That surely means you're nothing short of a heathen,' put in Hafwen, pursing her lips as she pushed another couple of tharcakes in his direction. 'Although I suppose you are *our* heathen.'

'These really are delicious!' he enthused, grinning at Meirian. 'And you've cut such nice deep crosses in each one to let out the evil spirits.'

'Evil spirits?' echoed Meirian in astonishment. 'Why on earth would there be evil spirits in oat cakes?'

'The blighters get everywhere,' he replied sombrely, raising his arms above his head and wiggling his fingers. 'Ask our old cook. *Whooooo* — '

'We'll have no more of that blasphemous behaviour, Mr Lyall,' interrupted Hafwen as though he were still a small boy. 'You may be full of the joys of spring, but the rest of us have work to do, so on your way and leave us in peace.'

'Actually, I came here for a very sensible reason,' he insisted, smiling across at Meirian. 'The water's gone down, so we could sail across Swallowhole Mere in complete safety. I was wondering if you'd care to come to Hermitage Island with me? It really is breathtakingly beautiful, even in winter.'

'You and James have told me so much about the island, I can't wait to see it,' she began ruefully. 'However, I'm going to the village with James, and my box is coming with the ferryman today, so we'll be driving out to collect that afterwards.'

'Of course; I wasn't thinking.' The ready smile couldn't quite conceal his disappointment. 'Perhaps we could do it another day. Whenever you're free.'

'I'll look forward to it.'

'It'll be my pleasure.' He paused in the doorway to the passage, glancing back at her. 'You'll be sure to keep the tharcake basket covered with the purest white muslin until you're safely within the confines of St Radegund's and all doors are closed?'

Meirian considered him warily. 'Dare I ask the reason?'

'If the basket's uncovered and the church doors are open, the wind will blow witches across the hills from Pendle, and they'll cast an evil spell onto the tharcakes to bewitch the villagers into serving the devil.'

'Obvious, really.' Meirian nodded, packing the tharcakes, half a dozen bantlings, and one of Haffie's special bag puddings into a parcel for Becky Beswick. 'I should've realised.'

'Not your fault you're unfamiliar with the weird customs of pagan Lancashire,' he answered blithely, helping himself to another tharcake and a hunk of crusty bread before disappearing into the hallway and leaving the two women to their work.

When the last of the carrots and parsnips were sliced and added to the pot, Meirian wrapped her shawl tightly about her shoulders and, taking the trug, quit the bright kitchen and scurried across the drying green to the fruit store. Although it was past daybreak, gloomy grey shadows still clung about the rain-soaked garden and wetness soaked up from the coarse grass into the hem of Meirian's thick skirts. Letting herself into the dry warmth of the fragrant storehouse, she withdrew a stump of candle and tinderbox from her pocket, and in an instant, soft light was bathing shelves and shelves of apples, pears and quince, all carefully set out upon trays so the one fruit did not touch the next and stored to last the household throughout the long winter months.

Meirian began collecting large thin-skinned baking apples first, then she'd need some of the rosy-red crabapples for jelly-making. James was partial to crabapple jelly with freshly baked bread and white cheese. And she mustn't forget sufficient sweet dessert apples for the supper table.

She paused, half-turning at a sound

outside. Supposing it to be merely a bird or foraging animal, she returned to selecting the apples, even as there came a tentative tapping at the low door.

'Annie!' she gasped, alarmed at the sight of the young white-faced woman with an infant bundled into her arms. 'What's wrong? It isn't the babe — '

'Oh no, miss. Nowt like that,' replied Annie hurriedly, her hollow eyes darting nervously over her shoulder and scanning the gloom of morning shadows. 'The bairn's doing right well. Emm's not half so fretful with her teeth after the remedy you gave her. I shouldn't have come, miss — I know it — but I . . . I've no one else to turn to!'

'Come on up to the kitchen straight away, Annie! You can get warm and have a hot drink. You're wet through.' Her brow creased at Annie's thin shawl and sodden homespun. 'You must've been out hours! Why didn't you knock at the garden door for me like always?'

'I'm not coming to the house!' she almost cried. 'I don't want nobody to see me. I — I've been waiting in the wood. For you to come out t'house so I could catch you on your own.'

'Whatever is it, Annie?' Drawing her inside, Meirian led her to the pile of clean dry sacks heaped in the corner of the warmly lit fruit store and sat her down, peeling off the soaked shawl and replacing it with her own. 'How can I help?'

'I'm not sure as you can, but I couldn't keep it bottled up no more. It's Billy. He's lost his job!' She raised troubled eyes to Meirian. 'He come home four days since and said the boss sacked him for no reason!'

Meirian hadn't ever seen Annie's husband. Upon the occasions she'd visited the family's cottage on Colletts Turn, Billy Wilcox had never been at home. 'Where is it he worked?'

'For Mr Coates up at the quarry. Oh, I know Billy has a mean temper on him, 'specially when he's had a few, but he swore to me he done nothing wrong! Billy said he'd been kicked out just so

Coates could give his job to one of his mates. When I asked how were we to manage on just my wages from The Swan, Billy told me to stop whinging 'cause he'd get summat else. But he *hasn't*, miss!' Annie shook her head in despair. 'He hasn't! Rent day's coming round again, and how are we to pay it if Billy's got no job?'

'I'll have a word with Mr Weir,' said Meirian quietly. She didn't relish the notion of asking Tod Weir for a favour, but he was in charge of hiring on outside workers for the estate. 'Now the floodwater has gone down — '

'No, please don't tell the baily Billy's out of work!' Annie cried out in alarm. 'Once Mr Weir hears, he'll turn us out of our home!'

'Surely not!' exclaimed Meirian. 'You're tenants of the estate. Tod Weir isn't your landlord!'

'He might as well be, miss! It's him as collects the rents and says who stays and who goes,' insisted Annie anxiously. 'I've seen it happen. Once folk are even a day late paying, he throws 'em out so he can give their cottage to one of his cronies — and get a nice backhander on the side!'

'Tod Weir does what?' queried Meirian sharply. 'You mean Weir accepts bribes to allocate cottages.'

'It's the way of the world, miss. Billy says it's not what you know, it's who you know, and he's right,' she cut in, getting to her feet. 'I'd best get home. Billy had a skinful last night and he's sleeping it off, but if he wakes up and sees I've gone out . . . '

'I'll come to your cottage later with more remedy for Emm and a bottle of Mrs Caunce's winter tonic for you.' Meirian considered her companion, following her to the door. 'You need to keep your strength up, Annie.'

'You won't breathe a word, will you, miss?' Annie murmured with a backward glance. 'For the baily has eyes and ears all over Blackthorn, and he'll take our home off us.'

'This will stay between us, Annie.'

promised Meirian gently. 'Away with you now, and I'll see you this afternoon.'

She watched the slight figure scurrying away through the trees before turning once more into the fruit store. However, as Meirian was closing the door, she glimpsed the burly figure of Tod Weir standing perfectly motionless some distance across the garden. A shiver of revulsion ran down her spine. How long had he been lurking there? Aware Meirian had caught sight of him, the bailiff inclined his head politely and melted into the depths of the wood.

★ ★ ★

Meirian dearly wanted to ask her cousin's advice about how best to help Annie, but bound by her promise, she could only pack a basket of provisions for the family.

'Haffie, what sort of man is Annie's husband?'

'He's got a right mouth on him, has

Billy Wilcox. He's not a bad lad, although he can be a bit too quick with his fists when he's rattled,' replied Hafwen, stooping to the oven and checking on the rich black bun. 'He was a field hand on the home farm until he had a set-to with the cowman. That little wifie of his is worth ten of the big lummox. She was a maid here before she wed Billy and fell for her second bairn.'

'Annie worked here?'

'It's a long while since. Long before Captain James went in the army. I remember it clear because her and Miss Rosamund — Doctor Poulsom's daughter — were of a similar age, and after the doctor's wife died, Miss Rosamund often stayed at the manor house.'

'I'd never thought about it before,' mused Meirian. 'That James and Lyall and Rosamund Poulsom — and Annie, too — must've known each other all their lives. Grown up together, too.'

'The missus and Mrs Poulsom had

been the closest friends and were godmother to each other's children, you see.' finished Hafwen. 'Little Annie was a parlour maid then, but she attended Miss Rosamund whenever she was staying here. Quick as a pin to learn, was Annie. Reliable and hard-working. She'd have done well in any household, if she hadn't wed Billy Wilcox. She certainly could've done a lot better for herself than him!'

★ ★ ★

Meirian dressed in her best and made ready for the Feast of St Radegund celebrations. After collecting the enormous willow basket from the kitchen, she and James Caunce went out into the stable yard where young Alf had the wagon ready and waiting.

'Shall I fetch Miss Meirian's box from the ferryman, Captain Caunce?' he asked, loading the basket into the wagon bed.

'That's all right, Alf,' replied James,

handing Meirian up onto the seat before going around and climbing in himself. 'We'll collect it ourselves. I'm showing Miss Penlan around that part of Blackthorn once the fair gets underway.'

Alf tugged the peak of his cap and disappeared back into the coach-house. The wagon trundled across the cobbles and around a wide path lined by old arching beech.

'In grander days, the Caunces and their houseguests and retainers would have driven along this avenue to St Radegund's,' remarked James amiably. 'On summer evenings, the ladies would stroll beneath the shade of the beech trees to church for evensong and their devotions. The family has a private gate into the churchyard.'

'Mmm,' Meirian replied absently. Ordinarily, she liked picturing how life at the manor house was in the olden days, but today her mind was fixed upon less fanciful matters. She was sitting rigid at James's side, absorbed in her thoughts. If Annie was right about Tod Weir accepting bribes, the bailiff would clearly have more to gain by putting the family out of their cottage immediately than allowing them a little extra time to pay their rent. Meirian glanced sidelong at James. He was the squire. He would surely resolve everything, but how could Meirian betray a solemn confidence?

They drove on in silence, the huge brown horse's hoofs thudding softly on the leaf-strewn earth. At length, the spire of the parish church came into view through the arching canopy of beech boughs.

'It's not like you to be so quiet,' remarked James. 'Not worried about the ceremony, are you?'

'I don't know enough about what I'm supposed to do to be worried,' answered Meirian vaguely, adding, 'Mind, I am a bit apprehensive. This is the first time I've represented your mother at a village event.'

'You're not representing my mother

— you're representing the squire's lady,' he commented wryly. 'We say a few inspirational words at the school, lead the children's procession through the village to St Radegund's, sit through one of Len Sutcliffe's blood-and-thunder sermons, and then stand by the door dishing out tharcakes to the parishioners as they leave the church. The bell peals, the Feast Day Fair opens, and that's it.'

'You'll have to make the inspirational speech,' she said firmly. 'I'm not saying a word!'

'So there *is* a first time for everything.' He grinned, keeping his eyes on the path ahead. 'You might like to spare a thought for me; this is my first official occasion strutting around surveying all I rule. My father would cut a real dash on such days as this. I — I can see him now, swaggering about playing the squire for all it's worth.'

'It can't be easy for you,' murmured Meirian, hearing the unexpected catch in his voice. They were approaching the squat Norman church and could already see and hear the great mass of people and activity beyond in the village. 'Could we go to Annie Wilcox's cottage first? It's on Colletts Turn.'

'Of course.' He eyed the basket. 'Does the family have an illness?'

'No, but the baby's teething and Annie's very tired and run down. I've been taking them a few provisions.'

'That's thoughtful of you. Annie's a good woman. But if we go there now, she'll still be at The Swan.'

'How do you know the times Annie does washing at the inn?' exclaimed Meirian.

'Annie's my neighbor,' James said with a shrug. 'It's my business to know.'

It was on the tip of Meirian's tongue to ask if he also knew that her husband had been unfairly dismissed and the family was in fear of being thrown out onto the street, but she merely replied, 'I shall go later, then, for I'd like to see her.'

'Later it is. Any other errands before

we go to the school?'

She nodded. 'I've some tharcakes for Becky Beswick, but I don't know where he lives.'

'The old codger has a cobby on the far edge of the village, a distance from the mill by the woods.' James drove past the stocks and away beyond the market cross out through the village and down along the riverbank. When they passed the windmill, he raised a hand and pointed. 'There's Becky's cobby, tucked away yonder in the shelter of the alder wood.'

The tiny round cottage was built from stone cobs and had a low doorway and a single window draped over with oilskin. It was the most primitive dwelling Meirian had ever seen. 'There's little comfort here for such an aged man,' she commented bluntly. 'It's such a lonely spot, too.'

'Becky likes his peace and quiet. He was born near the church, but he's lived out in the wood for as long as I can remember,' remarked James, calling the old seafarer's name. 'Ah, here he comes.'

Becky Beswick was pushing a barrow groaning with kindling, his gait awkward with the crudely carved peg leg. He raised his face sharply when he spotted his visitors.

'Get yourself over here, Becky!' James grinned as he strode over the stubbly ground to meet the old man. 'This is Miss Meirian Penlan. She's giving the Feast Day tharcakes this year.'

'I've seen her round and about.'

'Good day, Mr Beswick,' said Meirian with a smile. Meeting him properly for the first time, she could plainly see that Becky's wrinkled face was scarred with black powder burns, and his sightless eye was watering and closed against the sharp wind whipping in across the river. 'How are you?'

'Things could be worse,' he replied sourly. 'Although not much.'

'It's being so cheery that keeps Becky going.' James winked at the old man.

'Give him the poke, Meirian.'

She held out the bulging bundle. 'Mrs Caunce sends her regards and some tharcakes. Hafwen asked to be remembered to you, and put in a pie and one of her treacle cakes. She said you had a sweet tooth.'

'I'm obliged.' Extending a gaunt paw, he took the heavy bag and opened it. Taking out one of the tharcakes, he considered it suspiciously. 'They look different. Who made 'em? Not Hafwen?'

'I did, but I followed her instructions very carefully.'

'Hmm. Well, I'll try them. I'll let you know what I think when I see you next — If I'm spared, that is.'

'I'll look forward to that, Mr Beswick.'

'Me fayther was 'Mr Beswick'. You call me Becky.'

'Thank you, I will,' she said with a nod. 'Are you coming to the fair later?'

'What would I want to do that for?

Thieves and tricksters, every man jack of 'em! I have nowt to do with folk, missy. I don't bother them, and they don't bother me.'

'I understand that,' she replied soberly. 'Sometimes solitude can be a welcome guest.'

'Eh?'

'She means a cantankerous old blighter like you is best left alone,' said James, slipping a flagon of Jamaican black rum into Becky's capacious pocket. 'We're off to the school now, but come up to the manor house in the next few days and there'll be a day's walling waiting for you.'

'I'll be there.' He grunted. 'Rum do about Billy Wilcox being out of work and Christmas on t'way, in't it?'

'I hadn't heard.'

'Aye,' Becky said over his shoulder, shambling away towards his cobby. 'Few days since.'

James jingled the reins and started back along the curving river, smiling down at Meirian. 'You've made a very good impression on Becky — he's really taken to you!'

'Are you sure about that?'

'Oh, yes. He'd have driven you off with his scythe otherwise,' he replied blithely. 'You know, you're back and forth to the village so often these days, you should learn to drive the wagon.'

'I've never had anything to do with horses,' she considered. 'However, it would be useful. I don't like having to bother you or Lyall or Alf to drive me every time I need the wagon.'

'That's settled, then.' Manoeuvring through the bustling village, he turned at the market cross and made for the schoolhouse. 'Once we're finished here, I'll teach you. You can drive us out to the ferryman and collect your box.'

She nodded. 'James, about what Becky was saying ... I need to tell — What's *he* doing here?'

'Who?' queried James, following her gaze to where Tod Weir was emerging from the schoolmaster's lodgings. He cast an indolent nod in their direction before being swallowed into the noisy milling crowd. 'Oh, Weir. He and George Legh are friends. Drinking and gaming pals as well.'

Just the sight of the bailiff had agitated Meirian. 'Everywhere I go lately, he's lurking and watching!'

'He hasn't said or done anything improper, has he?' demanded James sharply. 'You must tell me, Meirian!'

'No, nothing of that sort,' she said impatiently. 'There's just something thoroughly unpleasant about him, James. He's always *there*. I spotted him hovering outside the open study window when your mother and I were in there talking. Then this morning when I was collecting the apples, he was in the shadows, just standing and looking. Now he's here at the school. But it's not Weir I want to talk to you about,' went on Meirian, having to raise her voice above the rousing cheers going up at their approach to the school. 'You see, when I was in the fruit store this — '

'What?' he interrupted loudly, inclining his head to hers. 'I can't hear a word!'

'Never mind!' she mouthed, shaking her head. This wasn't the time to discuss it anyway. She'd speak to James quietly later on. At least now that he knew Billy Wilcox had lost his job, Meirian could openly ask for help.

A final cheer of welcome rang out from the children for the squire and his lady as they passed an inscribed slab of sandstone commemorating the founding of the school by Marmaduke Caunce in 1514. Crossing the threshold and entering the long low-ceilinged room, it reminded Meirian of the school she and Dafydd had attended in Conwy. At the far end were the fireplace and a large pulpit-like desk, with rows of benches and forms set out before it. These were now filling up as the pupils clattered inside and took their places.

After calling the school to order, George Legh reminded the children of the origins of the Feast Day celebrations. Meirian had the opportunity to study the schoolmaster's demeanour, and was far from impressed. Legh's voice was unsteady, and he often paused as though struggling to find the words of his lesson. And she immediately noticed how badly his hands were shaking. So much so, he had need to grip the edge of the desk tightly in order to still them. Sidelong, Meirian considered his appearance critically.

To be fair, there was nothing slovenly or unkempt about the tall, gaunt man. His black coat was pressed and brushed and his high white collar impeccably starched and spotless. He must be how old, she mused . . . middle to late forties, perhaps? His hair was salt-and-pepper and he was not an undistinguished man, at least not to look at. His wife had been considerably younger, Meirian recalled Gladys mentioning. Was their age difference the reason Mrs Legh had run off with another man? Or perhaps life married to the village schoolmaster was too dull for her, for George Legh looked a pretty dry stick. His countenance was drawn and the long, thin face haggard and hollow about the eyes. Brought about by too many nights gaming until all hours with Tod Weir, supposed Meirian disdainfully. And by drunkeness. She could plainly detect the odour of strong liquor on his breath, and it disgusted her.

Formally introducing the school's honoured visitors, George Legh stepped aside and James strode past the desk to the front of the class, leading Meirian beside him. 'Good morning, children!' he announced brightly. 'Many of you will have already seen Miss Penlan about the village, and it is she you must thank for making this year's Feast Day tharcakes.'

James spoke for but a few minutes more before ceremoniously declaring the rest of the day a holiday; then, taking Meirian's arm, he went from the classroom. While the children watched wide-eyed through the open doorway, James made great show of withdrawing a small parcel wrapped in a scrap of woollen cloth and tied with flax. Raising it high so it might be clearly seen by all, he then stooped to push the parcel deep into the soft earth under the doorstep. At a word from George Legh, the children solemnly filed down the step and gathered outside.

'What's in the dolly-bag?' whispered Meirian as the boys and girls separated to form two lines.

'Peat, grain and a whorl-stone — that's a small pebble from the riverbed,' James replied. 'They're to keep cold, want and evil from all who pass over the step into the school.'

With the children duly assembled, he and Meirian led the procession from the schoolhouse towards St Rade-gund's. The jostling tide of people crowding the narrow lanes melted apart, clearing a path through the village for the squire and his lady, the school and their teacher.

James was smiling, acknowledging greetings and exchanging a few words with folk as they went along. Realising she was expected to do likewise, Meirian smiled and nodded too.

'What were you trying to tell me earlier?' he said in a low voice as they neared the lychgate. 'Was it about Tod Weir?'

She shook her head. 'You recall Becky Beswick telling us Annie's husband has lost his job? Well, the family is struggling to make ends meet, James.'

'Small wonder if Billy's not working. A family that size can't live on the pittance Annie earns washing at The Swan.'

'Exactly. The point is — ' She paused, choosing her words. 'I understand the quarry boss had it in for Billy Wilcox and sacked him for no good reason.'

James looked sceptical. 'How well do you know Billy Wilcox, Meirian?'

'Hardly at all, but since he was dismissed through no fault of his own, will you give him his job back?'

'I can't do that!' exclaimed James in disbelief. 'I can't dictate who Simon Coates chooses to employ.'

'You own the quarry, don't you?' she persisted. 'This Simon Coates is your tenant? You're the squire, for goodness sake! If you can't set right an injustice, who can?'

'Simon Coates is a fair boss, Meirian,' responded James briskly. 'If he's seen fit to sack Billy, then I'd wager he had good cause. Even if Coates *did* get rid of Billy and replace him with a better worker, there's nothing wrong with that.'

'Isn't there?' she hissed, keeping her voice down as they passed through the west door and into the church. 'Not even when a whole family will lose their home if they fall into arrears with their rent?'

'It'll not come to that,' returned James, drawing open the curtained door of the Caunce family pew so Meirian might enter before him. 'Billy Wilcox is young and strong, and he's capable of a decent day's work when he puts his back into it. He'll have no trouble getting another job.'

'Well he hasn't found one yet!' she retorted, settling into her seat and gazing unseeing out across the church as the congregation poured inside.

'Has he actually looked?' asked James tersely. 'There's plenty of work to be had around Blackthorn, Meirian, not least because of all the flood damage needing to be put right.'

'You're the squire, yet you'll not lift a finger to help a man who's been unfairly treated!'

'See reason, Meirian!' he muttered in exasperation. 'If Wilcox had had an accident or was sick, we'd obviously make sure his family was housed and fed and cared for, but that's not the case.'

'That's your final word, is it?' She glared at him.

'Billy Wilcox is fit and healthy. He has a wife and family, and it's his duty to get a job and provide for them. *That's* my final word.'

★ ★ ★

Meirian seethed with indignation as she sat at James's side during the service. How could a man be so . . . so blinkered? He had the means to set everything right but simply refused to do it. Rarely had Meirian felt such anger and frustration. Annie and her family were in real danger of losing their home, and Meirian desperately wanted to do something — but she was utterly powerless to help them.

St Radegund's was full, with late-comers having to stand crammed together at the rear, while the village children sat cross-legged on the stone flags before the pulpit directly beneath the fierce glance of Reverend Sutcliffe. He spoke forcefully upon the perils of temptation and sloth, his gaze frequently scouring the rows of hungry, fidgeting children engaged in their own battles with temptation.

When the sermon finally ended, the prayers said and the last hymn sung, the congregation remained seated while James and Meirian rose from the Caunce pew and proceeded down the aisle to the west door. There they stood, giving a Feast Day tharcake to every parishioner and child filing out into the chill December morning. Each woman and child bobbed a curtsey, while the men and boys bowed their heads before donning caps once more. Meirian considered all the gratitude and deference old-fashioned and positively feudal, but noticed with disdain that James appeared to take it all in his stride.

With the church bell pealing, the children exploded into a riot of shouts and activity, racing into the colour and clamour of the fair and eagerly devouring their tharcakes as they went.

While the Feast Day cakes were being distributed, Henry Poulsom had been chatting with Reverend Sutcliffe; now he sauntered over to the west door and joined James and Meirian.

'That's that over with for another year!' he remarked, adding hopefully, 'I didn't have time for breakfast. I don't suppose there are any tharcakes needing a good home?'

'Only a few, I'm afraid,' replied Meirian, offering the basket. 'They're a bit squashed.'

'No matter. A hungry man can't afford to be picky! I believe you did the honours making them this year, too.' He helped himself to the crumbly oat cakes. 'These look mighty good — which is a darn sight more than can be said for our schoolmaster.'

The stout physician inclined his head towards the rigid figure of George Legh walking very slowly and alone in the direction of the schoolhouse. 'Thought he was going to keel over during the service!'

'George was worse for wear today,' admitted James ruefully.

'When we were at the school, he was scarcely able to string a sentence together without stumbling over his words,' put in Meirian crisply. 'He reeked of drink.'

'He has been getting worse of late.' James met Henry Poulsom's eyes gravely. 'I've not seen him this bad before, not even just after Eunice left him.'

'It's the season, my boy!' proclaimed Henry, starting down the steps with them and lighting his pipe. 'Christmas and the New Year. A time for reflection, isn't it? The stirring of warm old memories and the prospect of another cold, empty year stretching ahead. It takes lots of folk badly, and I'll wager George Legh is one of 'em — for I've never seen a man with a pulse looking as deathly as he does today.'

'I've tried talking to him, Henry. He seems hell-bent on drinking himself into an early grave.'

'Aye. Told him myself only last month if he didn't mend his ways he'd be lining the coffin-maker's pockets before he's much older,' related Poulsom, puffing a fragrant cloud of blue smoke. 'The brass tacks of it is, George Legh just don't care anymore. As far as he's concerned, he's nothing left to live for.'

Meirian pursed her lips. 'That's as may be, but what sort of example is he setting those children? It's little short of disgrace that a man in his state should be teaching children that's if he's still *capable* of teaching!'

'If he isn't capable . . . ' She heard James's heavy sigh. ' . . . then I'll have to replace him at the school. But if he's still doing his job and the pupils are learning as they should, then George stays.'

Meirian's jaw dropped in disbelief. 'The man's a drunkard, James! You saw what he was like!'

'I know, I know, but perhaps Henry's right and the season *is* getting him down,' responded James evenly. 'You see George Legh as a broken wreck, but I see him as the man he was and might be again if given a chance — '

'A chance?' she cut in. 'What chance is he giving his pupils?'

Henry Poulsom cleared his throat tactfully, putting on his hat and starting away down the winding path through the churchyard. 'I'll leave you two to your deliberations. Have to see a patient about his gout, don't you know.'

'Hmm? Oh, aye. Right, Henry. See you later,' said James distractedly, his thoughts forming an idea as he took Meirian's arm and indicated the bench beneath the berry-laden holly. 'Will you sit with me?' When they were both seated, he continued, 'I agree George Legh's future depends on whether the children are being taught properly. Meirian, I want you to keep an eye on the school for a while. You were a governess in York, weren't you? You'll be able to judge if the children are learning all they should.'

'I was not a governess,' she retorted tersely. 'The Allens took me on as a nursemaid, James. I only showed the children their letters and numbers and suchlike as they grew a little older. I'm not qualified to do what you ask.'

'There's no other way,' he persisted earnestly. 'You've experience of teaching. You're good with children and they like you, I've noticed that. Besides, the squire's lady always has a special interest in the school. Pays visits, gives out prizes, that sort of thing. Actually, it was my mother who insisted girls should be allowed into the school and had a right to be educated alongside the boys. The very idea caused trouble — Reverend Sutcliffe condemned it from the pulpit — but Ma fought on regardless, and girls in Blackthorn have attended school ever since.'

'Good for her!' Meirian said emphatically. 'Mrs Caunce is very . . . *progressive* in her opinions.'

'You've noticed that, eh?' he said with a small smile, adding soberly, 'Ma's a strong woman by nature, and I suppose she had to become even stronger to cope with my father's weakness.'

They walked in silence through the churchyard and out to the wagon.

'I'll do what I can. At the school, I mean,' Meirian said quietly when James offered his hand to help her climb aboard. 'What if you don't like what I find?'

'I trust your honesty and your judgement, Meirian,' he answered simply, taking up the reins. 'I'll abide with whatever you decide.'

Moving away from St Radegund's, the wagon edged into the milling throng. The lane ahead, curving through the village out towards Colletts Turn, was lined with stalls and trestles and booths selling everything from pots and pitchforks to fancy wares, Eastern silks and sugar-dusted sweetmeats. Piles of barrels, bales and bundles containing all manner of goods were heaped against cottage walls and stacked in corners, and everywhere there were people. Vendors, merchants, journeymen, jugglers, players, card sharps and magicians swelled crowds and crowds of folk, local and foreigners, all come by road and river to buy or to browse the biggest fair in the calendar.

A stilt-walker loomed on the horizon and a girl in spangles over to Meirian's left was eating fire, while somewhere nearby amongst the crush of onlookers Morris men were clog-dancing, shaking bell-sticks and clashing antlers.

'It's hopeless, James! We'll be hours driving through this lot. It would be quicker walking.'

He nodded. 'We'll leave the wagon back at the churchyard gate. Should be safe enough there, even with all these strangers about.'

'There's no sense your coming with me to Annie's,' she said practically, clambering down and taking the basket of provisions. 'I'll be there in no time. You could be making your way up onto the road, though even *that* won't be easy with all the bustle; then we can get along and collect my box. I'm looking forward to using my own stuff again at long last.'

'I suppose it'd be best,' agreed James reluctantly, eyeing the heaving mass of movement, noise, colour and voices surrounding them on all sides. 'There's a rabbit track that runs from the back of Colletts Turn up past Erskine's Well and through the thicket out onto the road. Ask anybody and they'll point it out to you. Follow that track after you've seen Annie and wait for me by the fallen birch — you can't miss it. I'll get up there as quick as I can. Meirian!' he called after her. 'Be careful. Fairs are dangerous places.'

With a nod, she plunged into the crowd and weaved her way along until finally she reached the corner turning into Colletts Turn — and froze where she stood.

Shrinking back from view, Meirian watched Tod Weir striding out from Annie's cottage. The door was closed noiselessly from inside, and with a fearful sinking in the pit of her stomach, Meirian watched the bailiff disappear amongst the traders' tents before she sped across and knocked at the cottage.

The door was edged open by Annie's eldest daughter, Mally. Her face was white and scared. 'Oh it's you, miss!' she gasped in relief. 'We thought it was him come back! Come in, Ma's — '

Before the girl could finish, Annie furiously confronted Meirian from the confines of the dim little room. 'You shopped us!' she shouted, her eyes wet and blazing. 'I *trusted* you and you turned me in! The baily's just been here — he's throwing us out by Christmas!'

5

The Feast Day fair was over, packed up, and gone.

Holding the reins lightly between her fingers, Meirian drove the wagon down through quiet, empty lanes and out to Colletts Turn. She was anxious to make peace with Annie, and to apologise; for she had done nothing to help the family.

Taking a steadying breath, she drew up outside the cottage. Her knock was answered by Mally. The girl's eyes were wary, and she chewed the inside of her cheek uncertainly.

'Mam's not here, miss.'

'I hoped she'd be home by now.' Meirian smiled kindly at the anxious child. 'Will your mam still be at The Swan, Mally?'

'Oh no, miss. She'll have done there and gone up to The Three Crowns.'

'Annie's working at The Three Crowns as well?' exclaimed Meirian in consternation. Even taking short cuts across the fields, the big coaching inn on the Lancaster road was at least six miles' walk away. 'What is it your mam does there?'

'Scrubbing, miss. She helps in the kitchen an' all. Their usual woman is lying in,' explained Mally, her gaze fixed upon the basket Meirian carried. 'She's not too well, Mam said, so she'll be off a few weeks more.'

'I see. I'll meet up with your mother later then,' she replied, offering the basket. 'Can I leave this with you? There's a big jar of soup from the kitchen that should still be hot. Some bread and cheese and milk, and a jar of gruel for the baby. Have something to eat straight away,' finished Meirian gently. 'It's a shame to let it go cold, and I daresay it'll be late before your mam's home again.'

'Aye, miss. It usually is. Thanks, miss.'

Turning to leave, Meirian paused and looked back at the gangly young girl. 'When I was last at the school, you read from the Bible, didn't you? You read very well, Mally.'

'I like reading, miss.'

'Don't you go to school now?'

'Can't, miss. I've to look after the baby and Norah while Mam's away. The woman who used to mind them while Mam went to The Swan can't have them all day, so I have to. Dad said I'm too old for school anyhow and I should be working by now.'

'Does he, now?' remarked Meirian, her face set.

'Aye, miss. And I will be working, soon as we find somebody else to mind the bairns.'

'What about your brother? Joe's still at school, isn't he?'

'He's a boy, miss. But even he won't be going after this week,' went on Mally, shifting the weight of the basket on her arm. 'Dad's fixed him up helping the pot-man at the Pig and Whistle.'

Meirian only just bit back a sharp retort. She'd heard Gladys speak of the seedy little tavern a mile or so from the village, and how ruffians came rolling out swearing and brawling at all hours. There were a couple of disreputable ladies there too, by all accounts.

Bidding Mally farewell, Meirian climbed onto the wagon and started back through the village. Her blood was boiling. Billy Wilcox couldn't find work for himself, but he could get his seven-year-old son a job washing ale pots in a spit-and-sawdust grog shop!

Approaching St Radegund's, she paused so Dorcas might drink from the horse trough and was standing stroking the horse's rough neck, trying to calm down, when Becky Beswick came out from the churchyard.

'Good day to you, missy.'

'Hmm? Oh, hello.' She smiled apologetically at the old man. 'Sorry, Becky. I was miles away.'

'It's a rum do, in't it?' he observed, squinting up at the bright winter sun.

'About the Wilcoxes.'

'You've heard about Tod Weir threatening to throw them out of their home before Christmas, then? It's nothing short of wicked!'

'Nay, I weren't meaning that. Weir does that sort of thing all t'time,' replied Becky, tipping his hat and shouldering his spade. 'Nay, I meant little Annie slaving all the hours God sends while Billy's up at yon Pig and Whistle downing ale and playing pitch-and-toss with that horse dealer he met at the fair. Still, there's nowt as queer as folk, is there, miss?'

He turned into the churchyard and went back to his digging, leaving Meirian staring thoughtfully after him. She frowned. What on earth was Billy Wilcox up to? Where was he finding the money to drink and gamble? Or might his meetings with the horse dealer mean a job was in the offing?

* * *

'I'm just not sure, Meirian,' sighed Isabelle Caunce, fingering the rich ruby-red woollen swatch from the haberdasher in Liverpool. 'It's a frightful expense, and it's not as though I haven't several perfectly serviceable winter coats already. And of course, people would talk, seeing me out and about wearing this colour, when I was widowed only a year ago.'

'Folk will always gossip, ma'am,' replied Meirian, considering a sketch of the coat Isabelle had in mind. 'If they can't find something, then they'll make it up. This coat would be ideal for your trip to the theatre with Dr Poulsom. Warm and practical, but very dressy.'

'Do you really think so? I'd wear it when we all go Christmas shopping in Kirkgate, too. Then there will be all those seasonal visits to neighbours across the county. I'll want to look smart while I'm visiting, won't I?' She gazed longingly from the swatch to the sketch and back again. 'Hang it all! If tongues wag, let them! If I can't be gay and dressy at Christmastide, when can I?'

'Good for you, ma'am,' said Meirian, beaming. 'Shall I write to the haberdasher straight away?'

'You're an appalling influence, my dear. Yes, please do so with all haste! And have you ordered the lace collar and cuffs I chose for Hafwen? Splendid! She'll think them an extravagance, but Hafwen likes such things, so why should she not have them once in a while?'

'It's all arranged, ma'am,' said Meirian, snipping the thread on the stocking she was mending and packing up her sewing basket. 'If anyone wants me for the rest of the morning, I'll be in the study.'

She was finishing off the correspondence and sorting it ready for Alf to take to the post when Lyall looked in at the study door. 'Ready whenever you are.' He smiled, glancing at her cluttered desk. 'My word, are all those letters Ma's Christmas invitations?'

'Not quite,' laughed Meirian, surveying the neat little piles of letters she'd already written to Isabelle's friends and neighbours across the county and the list of those still to be done. 'There are some other things as well, but not many.'

'Ma's determined to push the boat out this year. I heard her telling Henry that since this was the first Christmas in more than eight years that her sons have both been at home, she was going to celebrate the season in fine style.'

'Quite right, too,' Meirian said, nodding emphatically. 'Christmas is a time for families and being together. If you're fortunate enough to have your loved ones around you, then that's something really worth celebrating.'

Lyall saw a fleeting sadness in her eyes, and impulsively touched a gentle hand to her arm. 'I'm so glad you'll be with us this Christmas. We're going to have a high old time. Music and dancing and wassailing in the Great

Hall, with the whole village and lots of people from further away coming to join us on the winter solstice, and then Christmas itself just for the family.'

'Will Dr Poulsom be spending Christmas at Blackthorn?' enquired Meirian. His name wasn't on Isabelle's list, but then the two were such great friends, perhaps the doctor didn't need inviting. 'It must get very lonely for him, living on his own like he does and not having any family nearby. He seems such a kindly man, too.'

'Old Henry's one of the best, and of course he thinks the world of Ma,' replied Lyall. 'Years ago, our two families always spent Christmas together here at the manor house, but ever since Rosamund left and married, Henry has spent the festive season with them in Carlisle.'

'Don't they ever come here?'

Lyall shook his head. 'Now I think of it, Rosamund's never actually been back to Blackthorn at all.'

'What's she like?' asked Meirian

curiously. She'd heard tantalising snippets about the girl from just about everyone in the household — even young Alf had fond memories of Miss Rosamund. 'Gladys told me she'd had a whirlwind romance whilst visiting an aunt in Carlisle, and that her husband is a very wealthy and important gentleman of law.'

'Jonathan Petherbridge is a member of the Bar. King's Counsel. Has a very distinguished reputation, apparently,' replied Lyall. 'Seems a thoroughly nice chap, too. Much older than Rosamund, mind you. Petherbridge is obviously devoted to her and to their little daughter.'

'You've met him, then?'

'He's had dinner here at the manor house, actually. Henry had been to Carlisle for his granddaughter's christening, and Petherbridge travelled back with him and stayed in Blackthorn overnight. He was going to a trial in Liverpool the next day.'

'It's odd that Rosamund doesn't ever

visit her father though, don't you think?'

'Not really. She does live a considerable distance away.' He shrugged, crossing the study to glance from the window. 'The sun's beginning to glimmer through the mist — it's a perfect day to explore the island. It'll be very cold though, especially on the water, so be sure to wrap up well,' he continued enthusiastically. 'I've already put rugs in the boat, and Hafwen's prepared a picnic hamper for us, so as soon as you're finished here, we'll set off!'

★ ★ ★

Clad in her thick tweed skirt and Hafwen's heaviest coat, Meirian was putting on her bonnet in the looking-glass beside the stairs when James strode by, still wearing his outdoor clothes and boots.

'Are you coming or going?' he asked.

'Going,' she replied into the mirror,

tying her ribbons tightly. 'Lyall's taking me over to Hermitage Island.'

'You'll really enjoy it. When it's shrouded with mist, the island's particularly intense and romantic — in the purest sense of the word.'

Meirian glanced at him, arching an eyebrow. James wasn't usually given to flights of poetic fancy!

'It's a very atmospheric place,' he protested, reading her surprised expression. 'All those ancient footsteps and devotions. Hermitage Island's always struck me as a particularly thin place, too.'

'A *thin* place?'

'Have you not heard of that before? It's a place where only the thinnest veil divides us from the people and happenings of the past.'

'Jolly robins!' she returned with a laugh. 'And people say the Welsh are superstitious!'

'It isn't superstition, Meirian. It's more than that. You'll likely feel it for yourself. Over time, so much has occurred out there. It's like the island is haunted by all that's gone before.'

'Not more ghosts and evil spirits!'

'No, they're all right here in the manor house.' He grinned, adding seriously, 'I can't describe it properly, but somehow when you're on Hermitage Island, shadows of the past are everywhere.'

'Ancient past or recent past?' she queried curiously, only to see an unexpected darkness cloud James's clear blue eyes.

'Here, don't forget your mittens.' He took the gloves from the top of the carved chest under the stairs. 'You'll be needing 'em today.'

Putting them on, Meirian turned from the mirror and started along the passage. James fell into step beside her.

'I had business up at Coates's quarry this morning,' he said evenly. 'While I was there, I asked Simon why he'd sacked Billy Wilcox. He had sufficient reason, Meirian. Billy lost his temper and caused ructions. Simon had no choice but get shot of him. I'd have done the same. You can't have workers thumping one another — not on company time, anyhow.'

'So you were right all along, and I was completely in the wrong?' She bridled, then caught a breath and sighed. 'To be truthful, the more I've seen of Billy Wilcox, the less sympathy I have for the man. Yet Annie has utter faith in him. Swears he's blameless and is doing his best.'

'He's her husband.' James commented simply.

'Much good he's doing, spending his days at the Pig and Whistle!' returned Meirian, adding bluntly, '*Will* you allow Tod Weir to put them out of their cottage if they can't pay the rent?'

'I know exactly what you're thinking, Meirian,' he said, pausing when they reached the great oak door. 'However, if we let Billy Wilcox off with paying his debts, when he's perfectly capable of earning a decent wage, it'd not only be wrong, it'd be unfair to all the tenants who *do* work hard. It isn't a pretty state of affairs, but that's the way it is,' concluded James, drawing open the heavy door for her. 'It was Billy's own fault he lost his job. Now it's up to him to shape himself up and provide for his family.'

6

Buttoning her gloves, Meirian hurried across the garden to meet Lyall. Wisps of chill white mist were draping the bare boughs of birch, oak and sycamore as they started into the wood towards Swallowhole Mere. The footing was slippery, and more than once Lyall took Meirian's arm to steady her on the rough ground.

'Wait until you see the picnic hamper,' he was saying amiably. 'I think Hafwen was worried we might be marooned and has packed enough food to last us a month!'

Meirian made to reply, but instead gasped as they emerged from the trees and she caught her first proper sighting of Swallowhole Mere. Suddenly, it was all too easy to give credence to the sinister legends. The mere was shrouded in vaporous mist, shifting and wavering above deep silvery water, thinning only to drift even closer and denser than before. Shafts of pale wintry sunlight shimmering through the haze glittered upon smooth ripples, lapping noiselessly against tall frost-blackened rushes. Meirian caught her breath, shivering at a gust of cold air sweeping across the still waters. In its wake, Hermitage Island gradually emerged. Through the stirring mist, its green banks, crags and the ancient stones of the monks' sanctum rose up, only to melt like wraiths, leaving the placid water and white lawny mist before her eyes.

'Although I've glimpsed the mere from my window,' murmured Meirian, awestruck, 'I'd never imagined it to be so . . . so . . . '

'Ethereal?' he put in helpfully, his smile warm at her response to the vista unfolding before her. 'Beautiful, remote, haunting?'

'All of those! And 'haunting' is the very word James used to describe

Hermitage Island not an hour ago.'

'It fits,' he replied, offering his hand and steadying the sculler when they reached the water's edge. 'There's a quality about the place that lingers, bewitching you and bringing you back here again and again. It gets into your very blood somehow. You'll see.'

'James said that too,' she laughed, clambering into the sturdy craft bobbing at the water's edge. 'This is much nicer than the last occasion I was in one of these funny little flat-bottomed boats.'

'I think you were remarkably brave to make that journey on such a stormy night.' He set the picnic hamper at Meirian's feet and handed the rugs about her before climbing aboard and casting off.

No sooner had they pushed away from the bank than the mist seemed to unaccountably thicken, obscuring the island completely. Within moments, all Meirian could see of land were disembodied skeletal branches reaching from the bone-chilling mist like grasping arms. Another few seconds and they, too, had vanished into damp cloying whiteness.

Meirian shuddered, aware of the same creeping, irrational fear she'd experienced in the Great Hall upon her first night at Blackthorn. The mist shrouded close all about them, clinging to her hair and touching her cheek with cold, damp breath.

'Don't worry, I could do this blindfolded,' Lyall reassured her gently, guiding the craft with strong, easy strokes. 'Keep the rugs about you. We'll soon be there.'

She nodded, common sense winning through and dispelling her apprehension. 'It *is* eerie, though. No wonder local folk are superstitious about Swallowhole. Gladys has told me some of the old horror stories.'

'There's no shortage of those.' He smiled. 'As with most legends, there's a grain of truth in most of them.'

'That the mere is the devil's work

and got its name because there's a hole in the water that swallows up witches?' she challenged wryly.

'Well, there *is* a hole, but it's a perfectly natural phenomenon,' replied Lyall, deftly manoeuvring the sculler. 'James could explain this far better than I. When he was a boy, he was really interested in Hermitage Island and read every scrap of information he could find in the library. You see, although the surface of the mere looks calm, there's one particular spot where an underwater current spirals down into the deepest water.' He went on, 'This swirling current sucks in whatever it catches and carries it away.'

'The mere's certainly perilous.' Meirian's gaze fell to the glassy surface of the water, and she tried not to think about their tiny boat being sucked down by a hidden current. 'But what has it to do with Gladys's tales of the devil and witches?'

'Centuries ago, Blackthorn and several other places in the county were rumoured to be rife with witchcraft. It's said whenever the witchfinder general came to purge Blackthorn and was hunting the women down, they'd flee to Swallowhole Mere and throw themselves into the water. But instead of drowning, they were carried underwater in the devil's arms and put safely ashore miles away.'

'That's not very likely, is it?' remarked Meirian scathingly, looking around the misty mere and only too easily imagining the women driven by fear into these deep silken waters.

'Agreed, and James put it down to propaganda to bolster the witch hunt,' replied Lyall. 'Then years later, he was reading one of our family's memoirs, and it mentioned how during the Civil War when there were battles in Blackthorn, the writer's grandfather and three other Caunce men evaded capture and certain death at enemy hands by diving down into the Swallowhole. They washed up some miles away, travelled by night down to

Liverpool, and sailed to the Americas. They settled in Virginia, made their fortune, and founded another branch of the family.'

'*That* sounds even more unlikely,' she declared emphatically. 'I used to read such adventurous tales to the Allen boys in York.'

'I admit, it is fairly far-fetched,' he laughed. 'But currents do sweep people for miles, though whether they'd wash up alive is another matter. Although if someone were desperate enough, then perhaps the gamble would be worth taking. So the story might well be true.'

Meirian nodded thoughtfully, and they sailed on without talking for a while. The occasional water bird squawked a protest at being disturbed by their paddling too close, and other ducks silently glided alongside the sculler for a spell before being absorbed into the mist.

Presently, ancient stones and blurs of greenery emerged from the haze, and the boat touched shore. After bringing the sculler up from the shallows, Lyall helped Meirian onto the pebbly shore, and they commenced climbing a steep rocky bank until gradually the hunting lodge came into clearer focus.

'I'd expected it to be tiny and primitive,' she gasped, breathless after the climb, and gazing up at an imposing entrance with large windows at either side and a row of four tall leaded windows gleaming with stained glass on the floor above. 'It's so grand!'

'Oh, the monk's hermitage is only this part over here,' said Lyall, striding over to the south corner and resting his palm flat against the soft weathered sandstone. 'It's little more than a cell. After the monastery was closed down in the 1540s, a Caunce brought some of its stones across to the island and built a hunting lodge onto the side of the hermitage. The monk's cell would've been used for storing wines and spirits then — hunting parties tend to consume vast quantities of both.'

Meirian wandered around the corner,

not wanting to miss a thing. 'And this is where you and James played when you were little?'

'The hunting lodge was almost a ruin in those days. It hadn't been used for years. Pa spent too much time in town and away visiting friends across the county to bother with the place, so we three had the island all to ourselves.' He smiled, offering his arm as they strolled. 'It was paradise! James, Rosamund and I practically lived over here — *did* live here during the summer-times. We'd make camp, build a fire, and only sail across to the mainland when we needed more food. When Pa decided to restore the hunting lodge, he didn't want us disturbing the fish and fowl or his guests, so we were forbidden from coming across to the island,' concluded Lyall matter-of-factly. 'Luckily, we were grown up by then. Well, Rosamund and I were about fourteen, and James was older, of course; so I don't expect we would've spent too many more sum-mers here anyway. Let's go inside. I came over first thing and lit the big fire downstairs, so it should be passably warm by now.'

'That was thoughtful of you.'

'It's a cold day, Meirian, and the old place is usually freezing. When I'm here painting, I tend to live upstairs, because the rooms are smaller and easier to keep warm.'

They began walking around the island; parts were thickly wooded while others were craggy and pitted with caves. Ponds lay hidden amongst the trees, with coots, moorhens and ducks gliding silently or hidden amongst the feathery rushes. On the flat slope of grassy vegetation a skein of geese grazed.

'It's surprising how quiet and subdued the birds seem when the weather's misty,' remarked Lyall when they paused for a breather on a high crag above a stretch of pebbly beach. 'I do a lot of my sketching up here, and walk when I'm thinking through my ideas. If it's raining, I take my sketchbook down into the mouth of the cave beneath our feet and work there. I'll show you.' He shinned down the rocky slope a little way, reaching up for Meirian's hand. 'Then we'll cut across back to the lodge. We haven't enough time to explore the whole island today.'

Once on the beach, Meirian would hardly have guessed a cave existed there at all had Lyall not pointed out the narrow opening concealed amongst the creases and crevices in the crag. 'Lyall, I don't want to pry,' she began tentatively as they began strolling back to the lodge. 'Tell me to mind my own business if you wish. I've often wanted to ask you, but there's never seemed to be a right moment.'

'About the dreams?' he interrupted gently, shaking his head with a smile. 'They haven't come for weeks now, Meirian. I'm sleeping better, too. I feel much better altogether, actually; far more able to cope with everything. I'm able to work without being depressed all the while.'

'I'm glad.' She smiled up at him, instinctively resting her gloved hand upon his arm for a moment. 'All things pass eventually — but that's no comfort when you're unhappy and life is at its blackest.'

He nodded, touching his own hand to hers as they walked. 'You were a friend indeed that night, Meirian. I'll never forget your kindness. I'm so pleased you were able to come with me today. It's wonderful to have your company for a few hours, away from the hustle and bustle of the manor house.'

They'd returned to the front of the lodge, however instead of turning into the arched porch with its dogs'-tooth carving, Lyall continued along towards the south corner.

'I prefer to use the monk's door; and besides, I want to show you the hermitage.' He pushed open a low incredibly heavy door set deep into the thick stone wall. For a moment they stood in complete darkness until Lyall lit a candle, holding it high so Meirian might glimpse her surroundings.

'This hermitage is where a monk would come to pray and be alone with his god. It could be almost a thousand years old,' he murmured, his eyes raised to the rough-hewn walls and roof. 'Think of it, Meirian — a thousand years ago, someone would have stood where we're standing, looked at these very walls, seen exactly what we are seeing. Isn't that incredible?'

'I've never been anywhere quite like it,' she replied quietly, impressed by the age and atmosphere of the sacred cell. 'It means a great deal to you, doesn't it?'

'It's my inspiration, Meirian,' he answered simply, meeting her gaze. 'When Pa died the way he did, I couldn't paint. Couldn't think straight. Couldn't even weep for him. Then one day I came here, for the first time in years. I just wandered around as we have this afternoon. Looking at everything, absorbing it all. And suddenly, I was impatient to paint again! I fetched my paints and got started straight away. However jaded and hopeless I might feel, as soon as I set foot on this island, the inspiration and the skill to fulfil it floods into me. My work has never been better, and it's all because of this wonderful place — '

He broke off, suddenly self-conscious, and shrugged apologetically. 'Forgive my rattling on when you've come for something far more interesting! Look, this alcove has shelves cut into the stones where the monk would've kept his books, and the tall narrow window faces south, so he'd have the best light for studying the gospels. This raised stone was his chapel and altar — see the five small crosses?'

'The five wounds of Christ.' Meirian traced the crudely hewn crosses at each corner and in the centre of the flat oblong stone. 'I remember Ma telling me she'd once seen such an ancient altar, but I never have before.'

'The monk would've offered his devotions here. That tiny crevice up there was for his candle, and the bowl-shape hollowed out from the wall was for holy water. Isn't it wonderful?' he said reverently, his eyes shining in the dull candlelight. 'Somehow, it brings out the very best one can give.'

Although impressed by the age and atmosphere of the ancient holy place, Meirian could not share Lyall's obvious passion for the dismal stone cell that clearly ignited his senses and inspired his work with such fervour. 'I wouldn't have cared to be alone here for months on end,' she remarked practically. 'It's so terribly isolated and lonely. But then, I daresay that's the whole purpose of a hermitage, isn't it?'

Her typically sensible attitude broke the sombre spell and Lyall chuckled, reaching for her hand. 'A door's been cut through the wall and into the lodge, over here. There are three steps up and they're quite steep and uneven, so watch your footing.'

Barely able to see where she was going, Meirian was glad to hang onto Lyall's hand as he led the way up a clammy stairwell barely shoulders' width across. Then the door ahead was pushed wide, opening onto the light and warmth of the hunting lodge's hall. A huge fire burned in the most enormous fireplace Meirian had ever set eyes upon, and she gasped in surprise at the rich floor coverings, comfortable furnishings and huge wall tapestries. At the far end of the hall, a wide staircase rose to a gallery with more rooms opening off.

'I imagined a hunting lodge would be spartan with bare floors and suchlike.'

'Pa insisted on his comforts,' Lyall said with a smile. 'When I came in for the first time after he died, I was surprised to find how neat and tidy everything was. I suppose Tod Weir saw to all those mundane chores for Pa. He organised just about everything else for him.'

'It doesn't sound as though there's any love lost between you and the bailiff.'

'I loathe Tod Weir,' he answered with conviction. 'I blame him for — for . . . He's a thoroughly unprincipled, despicable man! I'm certain Pa knew him for what he really was, but he had to depend upon Weir, you see. Weir ran everything at Blackthorn so Pa didn't have to.'

Meirian drew breath but said nothing. Moving to the fire, she warmed her hands. 'It's an impressive room.'

'Isn't it just?' he agreed, glancing around. 'Pa was a sporting man, as you can see. Not all of his trophies came from the island or from Blackthorn, of course. He brought that huge stag back from a shooting party in Scotland.'

There were otter tails and stags' heads hung upon the walls, stuffed birds and mammals with staring glass eyes hovered on shelves and cabinets, and several huge animal skins were spread across the floor before the fireplace, which was set around with great leather couches. The room was furnished with card and gaming tables and a heavily carved whiskey chest; and in the centre, beneath an enormous candelabrum, stood a billiard table.

It was undoubtedly a man's room, opined Meirian, standing before the fireplace and gazing upon a row of hunting trophies. Paintings of hawking, coursing and cockfighting adorned the alcoves and chimney corner. There was no feminine touch about this place, and she wondered wryly if the late Donald Caunce had barred his wife from visiting, in the same manner as he forbade his sons to come to the island.

Lyall stooped, taking another pine log from the alcove and setting it upon the fire. 'Shall we have our picnic tea now?'

'I *am* hungry,' she admitted. 'But actually, I'd like to see some of your paintings first. If you wouldn't mind, that is?'

'Mind? I'd be delighted!' he exclaimed,

starting across the room towards the broad staircase. 'Although I do most of my preliminary sketches outdoors — usually on that crag I showed you — I hardly ever actually paint outside. I do all my painting up here. I use the room at the south corner above the hermitage for my studio. It's big and has windows on three sides, so the light's very good.'

They entered the large airy room, and Meirian gazed in admiration at the unframed paintings propped against the walls; another partially finished work stood against an easel, and bundles of sketches were pinned up or lay scattered in untidy heaps.

'These are wonderful!' she exclaimed truthfully, wandering around and looking at everything. 'This one — it's the harvest picture, isn't it? I remember on the morning after I arrived at Blackthorn, your coming in to the kitchen and saying you'd finally finished it.'

'Fancy your remembering that!' he laughed. 'Yes, I'd really struggled with the tones and all sorts of other things.'

'It looks exactly as I imagine a harvest to be,' Meirian declared, lingering at the rustic scene with its golden glowing colours and lively faces creased with character and expression. At length, she moved along to a collection of quite different subjects. 'Are these your most recent pictures? There's a . . . a darkness about them I can't quite describe. It's quite disturbing.'

Lyall frowned in concern. 'Is that what you see? I do have dark moods sometimes, but I don't want people to see them in my work. Perhaps when I'm choosing which pictures to include in the exhibition, you'd help me? I'll leave any depressing ones at home.'

'I'd be pleased to, if you think I could be useful,' she agreed at once. 'You must be terribly excited about the exhibition. It's next month, isn't it?'

He nodded. 'I'm going to Preston next week to visit Ambrose Mather. He and his wife are my patrons. He's an industrialist who's already endowed various libraries and galleries in Lancashire.

'This exhibition is the chance of a lifetime, Meirian,' he said, his face glowing. 'Mr Mather is a respected patron of the arts, so his esteem and support are invaluable. Even before anybody has set eyes on my work, Ambrose Mather's patronage will open doors. I really can't afford to fail, you know. The rest of my life and my whole career depend upon the success of this exhibition. If it fails, there isn't anything left for me. Opportunities don't come along more than once in a lifetime.'

Meirian glanced up at him. For all Lyall's exuberance, she detected a strain about his eyes and an occasionally faraway brightness that troubled her. He must be under intense pressure. They continued around the studio, Lyall showing her the views from each of the room's three windows, telling her a little more about his pictures as they went.

Image after image delighted Meirian's senses, but her favourite was a painting clearly inspired by Lyall's childhood memories. It portrayed three children playing on the island's shore, with the old monk's cave barely visible beyond clumps of bright golden gorse. When she and Lyall had been exploring earlier, he'd shown her that very spot.

'The wild flowers and blossoms always seemed at their most colourful on those long-ago summer days, when we were all here together on Hermitage,' he enthused now, beaming down at Meirian. 'The water of the mere was the bluest azure you've ever imagined, too.'

'Oh, this *is* beautiful, Lyall,' she murmured, hardly able to take her eyes from the warmth and colour and vitality radiating from the painting. 'It *is* you and James and Rosamund Poulsom, isn't it? Why, I can almost hear the birds singing and the children laughing and calling to each other. It's such a wonderfully happy, carefree picture!'

'Is it? Is it really?' he asked tentatively. 'Do you really think so? Because that's exactly what I wanted this picture to convey. Paintings should stir the emotions and be evocative. Those days on the island with Rosamund and James were the happiest of times, before we started to grow up and first James and then Rosamund left Blackthorn. Everything changed then. It was Pa who changed most of all, though,' reflected Lyall sombrely. 'I don't believe he ever got over it. James had always been his favourite.'

They quit the studio and Meirian fell into step with Lyall, walking beside him along a wide landing with doors leading into the rooms she'd glimpsed from outside. Through one open doorway, she couldn't help but notice the master bedroom. The dusty furnishings, carpets and massive four-poster with its heavily worked curtains and draped canopy looked gloomy and neglected. Lyall observed her curious glance, and Meirian blushed.

'Sorry,' she said. 'I didn't mean to be nosy.'

'Oh, that's all right. Everything in that room is exactly as Pa left it upon the last occasion he came here before he . . . before he died,' finished Lyall firmly, going on, 'His clothes, pipes, books, rods, guns — all of his favourite possessions are still here at the lodge. Everything downstairs was his, too. None of it belongs to me.'

'I didn't think it was to your taste, somehow,' she replied gently.

'I should sort through Pa's belongings and remove them, but somehow I haven't been able to face it.'

'You'll do it when you're ready.'

'James is too busy to help, and I couldn't ask Ma. She hasn't been to Hermitage Island since the day I painted her wearing the amethyst necklace years ago. I suppose it's terribly weak of me not to have courage enough to get the task done, isn't it?'

'No, it's not, Lyall,' she insisted mildly. 'When my mother died, I was the only daughter, and she had no other female relatives close by. It fell to me to sort through her belongings. I did it straight away, thinking it best to get it over and done as soon as possible. But I was wrong,' went on Meirian soberly. 'Time heals, and if I'd allowed even a short time to pass, going through Mam's belongings and all the things she'd known and loved every day of her life would have given comfort. Instead, it was unbelievably painful and made my loss seem all the worse.'

'I hadn't thought about it that way,' he murmured at length, his dark eyes sorrowful as he gazed down at her. 'It must have been dreadful for you, Meirian.'

'It certainly didn't make a difficult time any easier,' she replied. 'Since there isn't any hurry to clear your father's things, why not leave it until you feel ready? The day *will* come when it won't be quite so painful.' Meirian added softly. 'I promise you that.'

'You're very kind, Meirian,' he said

awkwardly, his hand briefly resting upon her shoulder. 'You're the only person I could've confided in.'

'Perhaps it's something you need to have experienced before you understand.' She moved away slightly, warmth unexpectedly suffusing her face. 'It must be consoling to have so much of your father about you.'

'It is, actually,' he said absently. 'We were very close, Pa and I, especially when I was younger. Or at least, I was close to him. I'm not exactly sure how Pa felt. James was always his favourite, you see. Eldest son and heir, I suppose. Yet despite that, just before he left and joined the army, James turned against him.'

'Why? Did they quarrel?'

'They must have, I expect. I never actually overheard any argument or hard words, but James suddenly began ignoring Pa. You could have cut the atmosphere at the manor house with a blunt knife. Then without a word to any of us, James simply packed up and left

Blackthorn. It hurt Pa deeply. He never mentioned James's name again, and he never recovered from James's leaving either. It broke my father's heart, Meirian. I know it did.'

Meirian's own heart went out to the troubled young man. 'Having you at his side would have given your father great comfort, Lyall.'

'Yes. You'd think Pa and I would've been drawn closer, wouldn't you?' considered Lyall bleakly. 'But to be frank, he never had much time for me, Meirian. I never matched up to James in his eyes. In fact, James being gone just seemed to expose my shortcomings even more. Pa scorned my ambitions to paint, belittled my work . . . And when I offered to help him run Blackthorn, my father actually laughed in my face! He told me Tod Weir was the man doing it and that I should go back to my drawing books.'

A scathing indictment of Donald Caunce's behaviour was on Meirian's lips, but for Lyall's sake she did not give it voice. She doubtless should have held her tongue altogether, or at least tried to be tactful, but she was typically blunt.

'If your father did not value your talent as an artist, nor your worth as a man, then that was his loss,' she declared stoutly. 'Anybody would be proud to have you for their son.'

Lyall appeared not to hear, lost in the depths of his troubled thoughts. 'I daresay Pa would have preferred Tod Weir to sort his belongings. Weir offered the very day Pa died, but I told him never to set foot on the island again. I said Hermitage was to be mine and he was to keep away. Weir agreed, but I suspect he might've disobeyed me and come here anyway. I would never trust Tod Weir's word.'

'Why would he disobey you?' she queried. 'Would he wish to steal anything?'

'It's not that, I'm sure. Tod has no need to steal, for he's actually quite comfortably off.' Lyall frowned thoughtfully. 'No, it's more than that. I think perhaps he wanted to find something. He likes to have an edge, you see.'

Merian *didn't* see, and drew breath to ask Lyall to explain what he meant, however he changed the subject. 'Shall we have our picnic? I'm famished.'

Sitting before the roaring fire as the winter's afternoon closed in to dusk, they quietly conversed about the island and the lodge and Lyall's paintings. In the cocooning softness of flickering firelight, he reached across and touched her cheek tenderly. 'I'm so glad you came today, Meirian. I — I've never met anyone as special as you . . . '

The intensity in the depths of his dark eyes startled her, and Meirian dropped her gaze from his, fussing with her gloves. 'It's getting late,' she said brightly. 'We should be going home.'

'Yes,' she heard him say. 'Yes, I suppose we should.'

Meirian busied herself with bonnet and scarf, still feeling the gentle touch of Lyall's fingertips tingling upon her skin.

'You're never going up to The Three Crowns to see Annie tonight?' exclaimed Hafwen a few hours later when Meirian had said she wouldn't be in for supper. 'It's a long way, you know. And I was looking forward to hearing all about your trip to the island.'

'It was a lovely day, and I'll tell you all about it when I get back.' Meirian smiled as she put on her muffler. 'I need to speak to Annie, and catching her on her way home will give us the chance to talk by ourselves. I won't be late,' she finished, making for the garden door. 'Have the cocoa ready and we'll settle down for a right good chat.'

The mist that had lingered through-out the hours of daylight had dissipated, and it was a cold, clear evening as Meirian drove away from the manor house and up onto the Lancaster road.

There was no other traffic winding through woodland and out across open country. The rumble of wagon wheels and the steady thump of Bessie's hoofs were the only sounds; and as darkness deepened into a black moonless night, Meirian felt a prickle of unease. Footpads were known to lie in wait for hapless travellers. An unarmed woman would be easy prey indeed. A band of robbers would not know Meirian carried nothing of value.

The lantern swinging from the wagon cast but a dim pool of light down to the road ahead, and Meirian passed the journey peering beyond it to the ditches and bushes along the thoroughfare for any sound or movement.

The road followed a broad curve, and at long last the glowing torches of the large post inn appeared and illuminated the winter night. Meirian spotted a lone figure walking from the direction of

The Three Crowns, and at once felt ashamed. She'd been fussing about driving along the desolate road, while Annie Wilcox was making the same journey twice each day on foot!

Meirian raised the lantern. 'Annie! Annie, is that you?'

'Aye, it is!' came the reply as the slight woman drew nearer, her face lit by the lantern. 'Why, Miss Penlan! Whatever are you doing out here?'

'I came to meet you. Please, climb in.' Meirian offered her hand, taking up the other woman's bundle before helping her onto the seat. 'Annie, I owe you an apology. I *did* — '

'It's me as needs to say sorry, miss,' she interrupted with a rueful shake of her head. 'What I said that day . . . I don't know what came over me. Even as I was saying it, I knew it wasn't true. I knew you wouldn't have shopped us to the baily. It was just that when Tod Weir came banging on the door and barged in shouting the odds, I was scared.'

'With good reason!' muttered Meirian emphatically, driving on a little way until the road widened sufficiently for her to turn the wagon homewards. 'I saw Mally this morning. She told me about your temporary job at The Three Crowns and that Joe is starting at the tavern, but what of your husband? Rent day is coming up. Has Billy found any work yet?'

'He's not got anything just at the minute, miss,' she answered. 'But every week I put a few coppers by from my washing at The Swan — Billy don't know or he'd have it spent; he's never been one for saving. What with what I've got hidden away under the hearth and what I'll get from The Three Crowns, we'll be able to manage the rent all right this time.'

'What about next time?' persisted Meirian. 'Isn't the job at The Three Crowns only until the regular woman is well enough to return? What will happen then?'

'It dun't matter, miss. Thanks all the

same for minding, but Billy'll be fixed up and earning by then,' replied Annie confidently. 'He met this Irishman at the fair who buys and sells horses. He's not local himself, of course, and he was looking for somebody to do the trading round here and up Lancaster way. Anyhow, him and Billy got talking and had a few ales, and he offered Billy the job.'

'I'd heard Billy was drinking with a stranger in the tavern,' remarked Meirian doubtfully.

'That'd be him. The Irishman, I mean. Billy's been going to see him regular, to sort out all the details and such. He reckons he'll be starting work in a day or two, and he says it'll be paying a lot more than he ever got from the quarry. We'll have no worries about paying us rent anymore, miss — And as long as we pay on the dot,' concluded Annie triumphantly. 'Not even Tod Weir can chuck us out!'

★　★　★

It was later than she'd expected when Meirian finally got back to the manor house after taking Annie home to Colletts Turn. Hafwen had long since retired to her bed but had left a plate of pie, bread and cheese, and the makings of the cocoa ready for her cousin's return. While she waited at the fireside for the cocoa to heat, Meirian's weary thoughts strayed to her conversation with Annie. So Billy Wilcox had found himself a job after all. It paid well, and until his first wages came in, the savings Annie had squirrelled away under her cottage hearth would tide them over and pay the rent on Thursday. Why, then, was Meirian still fretting about the the family losing their home?

Giving herself a mental shake, she poured the steaming cocoa into a large mug and started upstairs with her cold supper plate. All of a sudden she was hungry, tired and cold, and longing for her bed. Carrying the laden tray carefully, she padded through the long gallery towards her room, pausing in her tracks at voices drifting clear as a bell up through the squint from the Great Hall below. She wouldn't have given it a second consideration, had she not immediately recognised the two voices: Lyall Caunce — and Tod Weir!

Meirian didn't intend eavesdropping; however, given Lyall's earlier remarks about the bailiff, for both men to be down in the Great Hall having an obviously acrimonious conversation at this late hour was curious to say the least. Taking a few steps nearer the squint, she noiselessly set down her tray and leaned forward so she might peer down through the peep-hole.

'I gave you the money and you promised you'd get it!' Lyall was saying agitatedly. 'Yet you come back empty-handed!'

'Ah, don't go getting yourself all riled up, Mister Lyall,' replied Weir soothingly. 'I can't get what isn't there to be got, can I now?'

'What am I to do, Weir?' demanded Lyall brokenly. 'What am I to *do*?'

'Be patient, sir. I know it's an imposition, but these things can't be helped. I'll be down in Liverpool again tomorrow. I'll see what I can do then. I'm sure I'll be able to fix you up as you want, but it'll likely cost. Maybe you'd prefer to leave it a wee spell longer?'

'How can I, you fool?' retorted Lyall distractedly, turning on his heel and pacing the echoing stone floor of the Great Hall. 'I must have it, however much it costs — do you understand?'

'I do indeed, sir,' the bailiff said smoothly. 'I'll ride to Liverpool with all speed at first light. Why don't you try to get some sleep? You can rely on me, Mister Lyall. Good night to you now . . . '

Hardly breathing, Meirian withdrew noiselessly from the squint, took up her tray, and crept to her room. Once within, she quickly undressed and climbed into bed, sitting up with the hot cocoa cupped into her cold hands.

7

Peter Lockwood was hefting the last of the churns onto the wagon as Meirian emerged from the dey-house carrying the butter and cheese.

'Thanks, Mr Lockwood,' she said, setting the basket onto the seat before climbing up. 'I was just saying to Patsy that we're looking forward to sampling her new cheese.'

'Aye, it's some fancy recipe she's concocted,' remarked the dairyman, glancing at his wife coming down the steps of the dey-house to see Meirian off. 'The old girl thought it'd be fitting, with Christmas coming up. I told her there's nowt wrong with proper plain cheese, but she'd not listen.'

Patsy Lockwood looked to Meirian in exasperation. 'If everybody was like my Pete, we'd be stuck in the Dark Ages! You be sure'n let me know what folk at the big house think of my new cheese. Tell 'em to try it with a nice tankard of pear cider.'

'I will.' Meirian raised a hand in goodbye as Bessie started away from the dairy. 'I'm sure it'll be delicious — it certainly looks it!'

Once on the road back up to the manor house, and with the last of the morning's errands done, she allowed her thoughts to wander. Despite Annie's confidence, Meirian was far from convinced Billy Wilcox would make good on this promise of a lucrative new job, and she'd decided to take matters into her own hands.

'Morning, miss!' called Alf when she drove into the stable yard. 'I'll be right with you.' Shinning down the ladder from the coach-house roof, the lad set to unloading the churns.

'How bad is the roof?' enquired Meirian, gazing up at the moss-covered slates.

'Gladys says she's got sieves that don't leak as much water,' he said with a grin, adding, 'It'll patch — until the next heavy rain.'

'Alf, how old were you when you started working here at Blackthorn Manor?'

He rubbed a calloused hand over his smooth chin. 'Can't say for sure, miss. I come with my two older brothers, see. I was about so high.'

Meirian considered. 'Seven or eight, maybe?'

'Aye, about that, I suppose. At first, I used to clean the boots and fill the scuttles and trim the lamps, chores like that.'

'You worked in the house?' she asked, surprised at such a young child employed indoors.

'Once I was strong enough, the baily put me outside. I like horses and I'm good with them, so when one of the stable lads left, I wangled his job,' he said cheerfully. ''Course, in them days there were loads of servants in the house and a lot more outside, too. That was before the old squire frittered away the last of the money, you see. Will there be owt else, miss?'

'No, that's all,' she replied thoughtfully, an entirely new notion occurring to her as she made for the kitchen. 'Thank you, Alf. Thank you very much indeed.'

The kitchen was unusually quiet. With the family all out and about until supper and no dinner to prepare, Hafwen was catching up with the household ironing. She found it soothing, when there wasn't need to hurry the job, and was humming softly when Meirian entered.

'Is Gladys about?'

Hafwen shook her head. 'Upstairs cleaning the parlour. Do you want her?'

'No, I wanted a private word with you about Annie Wilcox. Advice, really,' said Meirian seriously, quickly filling Hafwen in with the situation. 'So I was wondering how you'd feel if I took Annie on to help here in the kitchen. And young Joe for jobs around the house, too.'

Hafwen considered. As housekeeper, while it was right and proper her opinion be sought, it was for the mistress to take on the household staff. 'What does the missus think?'

'She's leaving it entirely up to me — about Annie, that is. I've only just had the idea of Joe for boots and suchlike. Mrs Caunce said if I could convince Annie the manor house isn't possessed by evil and persuade her to work here again, she'd be delighted.'

'We certainly need more help, especially with all the missus's Christmas plans. Annie would be an asset. Her little lad, too. The last house-boy went off with his mam when Cook saw the sprite,' commented Hafwen, carefully folding the table linen. 'Annie's a sensible lass; I'm sure she'll not be put off by all the silly tales!'

'I'll meet her on the way home from The Three Crowns again — ' began Meirian, breaking off in dismay. 'Oh, I won't be able to do that — I've to attend a parish meeting this evening!'

'And isn't it this afternoon you go in to the school?'

'Mmm. When I'm finished at the school, I'll go to The Swan for a bite to eat and stay there until it's time for the meeting,' she planned. 'I'll have to see Annie after that.'

* * *

Despite her initial misgivings, Meirian now found herself looking forward to the afternoons spent with the village children in the cluttered, smoky little classroom. Unfortunately, from the very outset, George Legh had been deeply hostile to her presence at his school.

'I imagine these visits are by way of hounding me from my post, Miss Penlan,' he'd declared stiffly upon that first afternoon. 'If I am to be on trial, I'd appreciate the courtesy of being told as much.'

'Whatever you may think, Mr Legh, I'm not here to condemn you,' she'd responded crisply. 'I'm taking an interest in the children's schooling on behalf of the squire. Providing all is as it should be, you need have no concern at my presence.'

In truth, Meirian had fully expected to find George Legh's teaching abilities sorely lacking in every respect. However, even by the conclusion of her first visit, the schoolmaster's thoroughness, firm and fair manner and endless patience with even the most trying of pupils caused Meirian to revise her poor opinion of him. With each subsequent visit, she came to appreciate what an exceptional teacher he once must have been, and perhaps — if James's optimism was not misplaced — could become again.

That afternoon, the children were having a spelling test. Afterwards, Meirian would read a story from the Bible and George Legh give a lesson about parables. The school scrambled to its feet in respectful greeting when Meirian entered and took her seat next to Legh behind the enormous desk. The schoolmaster called out the first name, and the spelling test began.

It was won by young Joe Wilcox, who had the honour of standing before the class and writing his name on the spelling ladder pinned upon the wall. Meirian opened the Bible and began reading, and the rest of the afternoon sped by.

Concluding the lesson, George Legh dismissed the school, and the class charged helter-skelter out into the December gloom. Meirian rose from the desk and put on her cloak.

'I understand Joe Wilcox is finishing school this week, Mr Legh,' she remarked, meeting his wary gaze. 'And his elder sister, Mally, has already left. They're bright children; it's a great shame they'll be unable to continue their education.'

'You concede children here are indeed learning, then?' he queried sardonically, his thin face set as he moved between the rows of benches collecting slates. 'It is a frequent occurrence, I'm afraid. Pupils, especially girls, leave school early because they're needed at home to care for younger ones. Parents take children from school and put them to work. Education is all very well in its place, Miss Penlan; however, far too many people think it's time wasted and doesn't put food on the table.'

'What do you think, Mr Legh?' she asked sharply, watching him neatly stacking the slates into the cupboard. 'What do you think of education for poor people and for girls?'

'I, Miss Penlan?' he enquired quizzically. 'Can you really have any interest in my views?'

Meirian pursed her lips, pulling on her gloves. 'I wouldn't have asked if I didn't wish to hear whatever you have to say.'

George Legh inclined his head slightly. 'Education is the key, Miss Penlan. Once a boy or girl possesses the tools of reading and writing, all doors in life might be opened.'

'Pretty sentiments indeed! Sadly, they don't wash with the likes of Billy Wilcox — ' she snapped, breaking off and taking a slow, resigned breath. 'My apologies, Mr Legh. I do agree with you. My parents were most insistent that my brother and I attend school, and it makes me so angry that any workshy father would send a bright little boy like Joe to wash ale-pots in a tavern of ill-repute!'

George Legh said nothing at first, replacing books into the cupboard. 'Your Bible stories appear to be making a considerable impression, Miss Penlan. I set the older pupils the task of writing upon the parable you read last week. And I've marked them.' He turned, meeting her gaze and offering a sheaf of dog-eared sheets. 'Perhaps you might care to examine the pupils' work?'

'I would, thank you.' Accepting the bundle, Meirian briskly went from the schoolhouse. 'Good afternoon, Mr Legh.'

'Good day to you, Miss Penlan.'

While she waited for the parish meeting to commence, Meirian settled herself into a quiet corner table at The Swan with a pot of tea, a dish of hot pikelets and gooseberry jam, and the bundle of schoolwork.

She read slowly and carefully, checking the children's spelling, the clearness of their handwriting, and their grasp of the story she'd told and the lesson George Legh had delivered afterwards. In particular, however, Meirian paid attention to the school-master's diligent marking. She was impressed, and still browsing the pages and sipping her third cup of tea when folk started arriving for the parish meeting. For the next three hours, all thoughts of the school and the future of its teacher were banished from Meirian's mind.

When she left The Swan, however, instead of driving through the village to Colletts Turn, Meirian crossed the green towards the schoolhouse with the intention of returning the pupils' work to George Legh and offering him some reassurance as to the security of his post.

The schoolhouse was in darkness, as were the adjoining lodgings. Legh was clearly not at home, and Meirian couldn't help but wonder if he was already out on yet another drinking spree. Letting herself into the dark, empty classroom, she lit the candle; and after placing the papers upon his desk, found pen and ink to write a brief covering note confirming her satisfaction with the pupils' work. On impulse, Meirian added a footnote expressing her interest and enjoyment of her regular visits to the school.

Snuffing the candle and going out, she closed the door behind her and turned only to bump into Tod Weir. A cry of alarm escaped Meirian's lips before she had chance to check it.

'Wisht, Miss Penlan!' he murmured silkily, gripping her arm as though to steady her. 'There's no cause to be afraid. 'Tis only myself.'

'You startled me, Mr Weir,' she returned, shaking free. 'That's all.'

'Ah, well I'm glad to hear it.' He tipped his hat, a sly grin spreading across his heavy features. 'To be honest, miss, I was a bit startled too, seeing you here at this late hour. Still, I suppose you and the good Mr Legh are very busy with matters of *education*.'

'I had the children's — '

However, Tod Weir was already gone, hands in pockets and whistling tunelessly. Meirian bridled at the bailiff's thinly disguised accusation of impropriety and worse. She could've kicked herself for even attempting to defend her presence at the schoolhouse!

Returning to The Swan and collecting Bessie and the wagon, she drove out to Colletts Turn and was relieved find Annie alone.

'Hello, miss! Come along in.' A smiled. 'I've not long got home seen Mally off to her bed. It's day for the lass, looking out for the bairns.'

'I'm sorry to call so late, but it's important.'

Annie's brow creased. 'Is owt wrong? It's not Billy — ?'

'No, no; just the opposite, really,' she interrupted swiftly. 'Mrs Caunce wishes to offer you a position at the manor house, helping Hafwen in the kitchen, and upstairs too. There'd also be a place for Joe,' added Meirian, choosing her words. 'He'd be working mostly in the house. It might be better for him in the long run than washing pots at — '

'I'll be the judge of that, Miss Penlan.'

Both women spun around to see Billy Wilcox's muscular frame filling the rear doorway.

'Billy love, you give us a right fright!' exclaimed Annie with a tense little laugh. 'We didn't hear you coming in.'

'I reckon you didn't.' He strode all the way inside, shutting the door behind him and seeming to fill the low, dimly lit kitchen. 'When I saw the horse and wagon out front, I wondered what business you had here at this hour.'

'I came for a word with Annie, Mr Wilcox,' she replied stiffly.

'I heard, and the answer's no. When she worked up there last time, she got ideas. I'll not have any wife of mine getting ideas above herself.'

'That's as may be,' said Meirian evenly, noticing Annie's increasing agitation as her gaze darted from one to other of their faces. 'Surely it's for Annie to decide — '

'She's my wife and it's my son — for I heard your fancy plans for him — and I've said no,' he cut in, looming above her in the cramped room. 'What I say goes, Mistress Penlan, so you can take yourself back where you come from.'

Meirian held her nerve. 'Mr Wilcox, rent day is coming up. Your wife is working herself into an early grave doing two — '

'Please, miss!' cried Annie desperately, her eyes large and fearful. 'Thanks all the same, miss. I'm obliged. But you'd best go.'

'This isn't — ' began Meirian, then bit her tongue and rose from the table. 'Of course. Good night, Annie. Mr Wilcox.'

8

'You did all you could, Meirian,' Lyall was saying on Thursday morning when they were up in his studio on Hermitage Island. 'If Billy Wilcox refuses to let Annie work at the manor house, there isn't anything more to be said.'

'It doesn't make sense, though!' she muttered in exasperation. They were carefully wrapping cotton sheets about each painting before adding a thick layer of sacking, to protect the pictures on their journey to Preston for framing. 'I doubt the existence of this grand new job he's supposed to have with the Irish horse dealer, so why wasn't Billy Wilcox glad for his wife to be offered a decent position earning good wages?'

'Perhaps there *is* a new job,' reasoned Lyall, tying a double knot while Meirian held the string taut. 'Or perhaps Wilcox just wants his wife where he can keep an eye on her. If Annie's all the way up at the manor house with a well-paid job, she's won't be so dependent upon him. Perhaps he doesn't want that to happen. Pride or something of the sort.'

'Hmm, he's certainly the type who'd want to keep his wife well and truly under his thumb!' declared Meirian grimly.

'It's rent day today, isn't it?' asked Lyall, wrapping another painting. 'Will Annie be able to pay?'

Meirian nodded. 'She has a little money hidden away and has been working all the hours God sends to make up enough for today's rent. What happens next rent day depends entirely upon whether Billy's fine new job is real or jolly robins.'

It was several more hours and umpteen trips back and forth across Swallowhole Mere before all of the paintings Lyall intended taking with him to Preston were safely packed and stacked in the drawing-room, ready for removal the following morning.

'Mr Mather has arranged a special carrier to take them into Preston,' Lyall told her when they were sharing a well-earned pot of tea before the fire. 'I'll be riding along with them, to make sure none of the paintings get damaged.'

'What's this Mr Mather like?' queried Meirian, watching him spear a thick slice of bread onto the toasting fork. 'He must be very wealthy.'

'I believe he has factories all over Lancashire,' commented Lyall, leaning towards the glowing coals. 'He seems a canny man, not at all the sort you'd imagine would be interested in art and literature; yet he's helped quite a few painters and poets. I met his wife and daughters last time I was in Preston, and they told me Mr Mather had put the money up for a lending library as well as endowing the wing at the gallery where my exhibition is being held.'

'And you're to be staying at their

home? How long will you be in Preston?'

'I'm not certain, but I shall be home before Christmas,' he replied. 'After my paintings are framed, Mr Mather wants to look at them all and decide which will make most impression upon the critics and dealers he's inviting to the exhibition. Then he's having a catalogue printed.'

'It sounds very businesslike. Not quite what I imagined, somehow.'

'I get a bit overwhelmed myself,' conceded Lyall, his face glowing with excitement and enthusiasm. 'But I've never been happier, Meirian! All I've ever wanted is to paint. The Mathers are making possible things I'd hardly dared dream about, and I have to make a great success of it. I *must* — for I'll never get a second chance!'

* * *

Dusting toast crumbs from her skirt, Meirian presently left the drawing-room and made her way to the screen passage outside the Great Hall. Tod Weir was seated at the long table collecting the manor's rents, the tenants' book open before him with a candle burning alongside. In a single glance, Meirian saw Mally Wilcox was not among the line of tenants waiting patiently to pay their dues, and wondered anxiously if the girl had already been and gone. As if reading her thoughts, the bailiff glanced up from marking the book and counting coins into the coffer-box.

'Your friends haven't shown up, miss,' he remarked smugly. 'If the rent's not paid by the fourth strike of St Radegund's clock, they're in arrears.'

'There's time enough yet,' was all Meirian said, turning on her heel and striding stiff-backed from the Great Hall. Once from the bailiff's sight, however, she ran to the stable yard.

'Alf! You were in the village earlier, weren't you? Have you heard anything of Annie Wilcox? Or Mally?'

He scratched his ear. 'Uh-uh, miss. Is owt wrong?'

'I hope not.' She glanced up at the sky. The afternoon was already closing in. Once the church clock struck four, Tod Weir would delay not a moment in sending his men to evict Annie and her family . . . Meirian's mind raced. Why hadn't their rent been paid? Annie would've gone to her work and entrusted the task to Mally. But what if the girl had been taken poorly? Or if one of the younger children was ill, and Mally couldn't leave them unattended?

'Alf, would you harness Bessie up for me? I must go down to the village directly!'

The beech avenue was the quickest route, and as Bessie drew the wagon down towards St Radegund's, Meirian heard the church clock striking the quarter hour. She was going around the village towards Colletts Turn when she spotted Mally, running for all she was worth past the stocks and up in the direction of the manor house.

'Mally! *Mally!*'

The girl swung around, running to Meirian. 'Oh, miss!' she gasped breathlessly, her words tumbling one over another. 'Mam told me to take the rent to the baily as soon as I had the bairns settled with Joey. I was getting the tin from under the hearth, but Dad come in and saw me and — and he took it all, miss!'

'Is your dad at home now, Mally?'

'Dunno where he is, miss, but I promised Mam about the rent — '

'It's going to be all right, I promise,' Meirian reassured her firmly, drawing Mally up onto the wagon. 'What of the little ones? Is somebody minding them?'

'Joe's with 'em, and he knows to knock at Mrs Lathom if he needs owt.'

'Right. We'll go and pay the rent.' She drove around the churchyard toward the beech avenue, glancing up to the old clock face. Tod Weir would close the book upon the stroke of four. There was no time to lose. 'I don't have any money on me, but I've enough saved at the manor house.'

The wagon trundled into the yard with only minutes to spare, and Meirian was sprinting across the cobbles to the garden door when she spotted James beside the well talking to Becky Beswick.

'James!' She ran to him, blurting. 'Can you lend me some money? I need it *now*, but my purse is upstairs in my room!'

'Meirian, take it easy!' he exclaimed. 'Whatever's wrong?'

'I'll explain later! Have you the money — ?'

The Great Hall was empty save for the bailiff up at the high table. The candle was burning low, the pen and ink pushed aside, but the tenants' book still lay open. Meirian lay the money down before him. 'The Wilcox rent. I'd be obliged if you'd enter it at once.'

'My, my, you've made it by the skin of your teeth, Miss Penlan! But with respect, you shouldn't be doing this, y'know.' He tutted reproachfully, signing off the tenants' book and closing it with a dull thump as the clock of St Radegund's struck the hour. 'Paying their rent out of your own pocket indeed! And will you be doing the same next rent day?'

'There'll be no need,' she retorted with a confidence she scarcely felt. 'For Mr Wilcox has found a job that pays well.'

The bailiff snorted. 'Believe that, miss, and you'll believe anything.' He rose, handing her the tenants' book and the coffer-box. 'Returned to your safekeeping, all added up and noted. They're quite heavy; would you not like me to carry them to the study for you?'

'That won't be necessary,' she returned icily, annoyed he'd fallen into step beside her as she started from the Great Hall.

'When I was collecting the book and box this morning, I noticed you've made the study into quite your own little nest.' He paused in the doorway, momentarily blocking her progress. 'I have to say Captain Caunce doesn't seem to mind sharing the accommodations at all. But then,' the bailiff added over his shoulder as he started away, 'the squire has always had a fine appreciation of a fair face and a shapely ankle.'

Fuming, Meirian hastily replaced the tenants' book and coffer-box into the study before running outdoors to tell Mally all was well and take the girl home to her family.

★　★　★

It was long past dark when Meirian finally returned to the manor house, slipping through the kitchen and upstairs to wash and change for supper. It would be the last evening the family would eat together for a while, because Lyall was leaving for Preston on the morrow.

Adjusting her cuffs as she passed the amethyst necklace portrait and hurried downstairs, Meirian could hear voices and laughter from the Great Hall. A great draught of cold air was rushing along the screen passage and she turned the corner to see James and Becky Beswick, Lyall and Alf dragging the biggest log she'd ever seen across the stone flags and around into the Great Hall.

'Our Yule log!' Lyall grinned as he glanced across at her. 'It's a bit heavy. You wouldn't care to give us a hand?'

'If I hadn't just changed for supper, I'd have been glad to!' she laughed, wandering into the Great Hall. It already appeared quite transformed; illuminated with great branches of candles, the very first fire she'd ever seen lit there burned and crackled in the huge hearth, and everywhere was the sharp, clean scent of pine needles and resin. 'It's going to look beautiful.'

'This will be the first Christmas we've celebrated in the Great Hall for many years,' murmured Isabelle Caunce, joining Meirian. 'And what a splendid Yule log Becky has found for us.'

'Aye, it's starting to feel like Christmastide,' said Becky, straightening up for a breather. 'It's high time the old hall saw some cheer again. It used to fair ring out in times past.'

'So it will again! We'll make this our best Christmas yet,' declared Isabelle, patting the elderly man's shoulder as she turned to leave. 'I'm relying on your flute playing for our Yule night, Becky. Oh, and before you go home, remember to look in at the kitchen. Hafwen will have a hotpot all ready and waiting.'

Meirian made to follow her from the Great Hall, but Becky caught her arm. 'It was a nice thing you did today, missy. For Annie and her bairns.'

'How did you — ' began Meirian, not bothering to finish. For all Becky Beswick lived like a hermit, it seemed very little happened in Blackthorn that the old man didn't know about. 'Becky, is there any truth in this job Billy

Wilcox says he has?'

'Happen,' replied Becky, rasping the whiskers on his cheek with a weathered palm. 'He's allwus in the Pig and Whistle with the hoss man. That's wun he's been all day today, so I heared.'

'Spending his family's hard-saved money,' muttered Meirian, nodding her thanks before leaving the men to their work.

It wasn't until after supper when she was in the study planning her next school visit, and James joined her, that Meirian had opportunity to return the money she'd borrowed.

'Is everything all right?' enquired James easily, stretching out in his favourite chair. 'You were unusually quiet at supper.'

'I had things to think about,' she answered, taking the purse from her pocket and offering the coins. When he wordlessly refused them, Meirian persisted, 'Please take it, James. You must.'

Inclining his head in resignation, he

accepted the money. 'I was glad to be able to help.'

'You saved the day,' she said simply, adding crisply, 'I suppose Tod Weir has told you why I needed it? And I suppose you agree it was a wrong thing to do?'

'Misguided, perhaps,' he conceded. 'Other tenants will resent it, and Billy Wilcox is the type who sees kindness as a weakness; however, you acted from concern for Annie and her family, and your compassion cannot be faulted.'

'She *had* saved enough money, James! Billy found it and took it.'

James merely nodded, saying nothing more as he leaned back in the winged chair and considered the array of schoolbooks on the desk before her. 'You're putting a lot of effort into these visits, aren't you? Do you reckon George Legh *will* need replacing?'

'Despite his fondness for drink, Mr Legh is perfectly competent,' she replied carefully. 'I've found no fault with his manner or his methods.

Indeed, I have been most favourably impressed. I'd like to continue visiting the children and reading them stories, though, if you have no objections?'

'Watching over the school is traditionally the domain of the squire's lady.' He smiled across at her. 'I'm glad about George. He's a good man.'

'A sad and lonely one, too,' she said ruefully. 'I fancy it's only his meticulous attention to his work that's holding him together — ' She broke off at the urgent rap upon the study door, swiftly followed by Gladys's anxious face peeping around the jamb.

'Sorry to disturb you, sir.' She bobbed to James and looked to Meirian. 'Annie Wilcox is at the garden door. She's in a right state — I think you'd best come!'

Sensing the maid's agitation, Meirian exchanged a glance with James and rose, but he stayed her arm. 'Bring Annie in here, Gladys,' he said quietly. 'I daresay some tea wouldn't go amiss, either.'

A few minutes later, Annie was ushered into the comfortable study, her head bowed. The bruised cheek and cut lip told their own story. Meirian was at once on her feet, drawing the other woman to the warmth of the fireside.

'He'd had a skinful, miss,' she murmured wearily. 'Come in wanting to know where else I'd hid money. I told him there was no more, but he'd not listen. I chased the bairns over to Mrs Lathom, and as soon as I got t'chance, I run out myself.'

Gladys entered meekly, setting down the tea. 'Will there be owt else?'

'Aye, there will,' James said, his eyes hard and cold. 'Make up one of the old maids' rooms. Annie'll be staying here tonight.'

'I can't stay, sir!' protested Annie, her startled eyes darting to his face. 'My bairns — '

'Still with Ma Lathom, are they?' he cut in, looking over to where Gladys was hovering. 'Tell Alf to take the wagon and fetch the children up here.

Is that all right with you, Annie?'

'Aye, sir, it is! And, miss,' she said, turning hesitantly to Meirian, 'if it's still going, I'd like that position you offered me. I wanted it all along.'

'I understand, Annie, but what will your husband say?'

'I've the bairns to think about, miss. I'll not have them made homeless while I can work to put a roof over their heads,' she said evenly. 'If the position's still going, I'll take it and be grateful.'

'Where's Billy now?' asked James grimly, rising and reaching for his coat. 'Still at your cottage?'

'James!' Meirian was instantly at his side, a knot of alarm tightening within her. 'What are you going to do?'

'Find Billy Wilcox,' he answered tersely, striding from the study. 'See how he likes squaring up to somebody who can fight back.'

'No! You can't — ' But he was already gone, the great oak door shutting loudly behind him.

* * *

The following hours passed in a flurry of activity. Annie's wounds were bathed and soothed, and when Alf arrived with the children, the family ate their fill at Hafwen's table before settling into one of the long-since occupied rooms amongst the servants' quarters.

When quietness settled once more upon the manor house, Meirian took her quilt and candle down into the Great Hall. It was fragrant with pines, and warm and bright from the Yule fire that would burn continuously throughout the festive season. Standing her candle jar upon the ledge and wrapping her quilt about her, she curled up on the settle next to the window overlooking the stable yard, her hand cupping her chin as she gazed through the leaded panes out into the winter night.

She wouldn't rest until she heard his horse's hoof beats and saw James home safe and sound.

9

'So Mally and Joe are working up at Blackthorn?' remarked George Legh when school was on its dinner break and Meirian was packing up after her visit. 'Mally is of an age when she'd likely be going into service anyway; and as for young Joe, at least this is a decent start to his working life, albeit a very early one!'

'Nonetheless, I agree with you, Mr Legh. They both should still be in school. However, what with their father deserting the family . . . '

'Has there been no word of Mr Wilcox's whereabouts?'

'Neither sight nor sound,' replied Meirian, not adding that upon that turbulent night, she'd been incredibly relieved when James finally returned to the manor house after a fruitless search for Billy Wilcox. When she and James had accompanied Annie to Colletts Turn the following day, it was to discover Billy's belongings gone and the tiny cottage in disarray. After Annie fled, he'd clearly ransacked their home looking for hidden money.

'It *is* going to be a struggle for Annie, but she's better off on her own than — ' Meirian broke off awkwardly, a deep flush creeping to her cheeks. 'I'm so sorry, Mr Legh! I didn't mean to — to . . .'

'I know you didn't, Miss Penlan,' he put in mildly, adding soberly, 'It's hardly a secret my wife deserted me, and I assure you there is no cause to avoid mentioning her or my marriage. Indeed, often I would welcome the liberty to speak of Eunice. One can become accustomed to being alone, although I doubt I shall ever be content with the solitary situation. I still love Eunice, you see. I always will.'

An unexpected lump came to Meirian's throat, moved that the lonely schoolmaster should confide so humbly and openly to her.

'How is Mrs Wilcox?' he asked after a moment. 'I haven't seen her in the village for several days.'

'After what happened, Annie was afraid to be at Colletts Turn in case Billy came back, so she and the children are staying up at Blackthorn for the time being,' replied Meirian. 'There's an old gamekeeper's cottage in the woods a short distance from the manor house. It's been empty a long while and needs repair. Alf and Becky are fixing it up so Annie and her family can move in. It's not very big, but they'll be safe there.'

'Quite so. I heard Mrs Wilcox had been hurt.'

'I hope never to set eyes upon Billy Wilcox again!' Meirian said emphatically, making ready to leave before the children came back inside for their afternoon's lessons. 'Mr Legh, I wonder if I might borrow some books for Mally? Joe's a bright child too, but I doubt he'd study in his spare time, whereas I'm certain Mally would welcome the chance to continue with her reading.'

'I'm sure she would.' He smiled. 'As for Joe . . . Boys his age seldom relish learning. He may return to education when he's a little older. Meanwhile, I'll choose a selection of books for Mally and pass them along to you.'

* * *

Hurrying through the kitchen where Annie was ironing and Mally helping Hafwen with the bread-baking, Meirian bumped into Isabelle at the foot of the stairs, making ready to go out.

'What do you think of the new coat?' she asked, fussing with the high collar. 'Does it look all right?'

'It's lovely!' exclaimed Meirian, admiring the neat style and deep rich ruby colour. 'Perfect for a wintry trip.'

'It'll certainly be wintry! We'll be on the coast road into Liverpool, and the wind whips straight across from the

Welsh mountains,' said Isabelle, buttoning her collar. 'Oh, we've had a letter from Lyall. Everything in Preston is splendid, and he's delighted with the picture-framing man. Anyhow, you can read it for yourself. Pass it along to James when you've finished. There's one for you from Lyall, too. He — '

'Isabelle! Is there any possibility of your being ready in the near future?' enquired Henry Poulsom in exasperation, appearing through the oaken door. 'The opera *is* this evening, you know.'

'I'm coming, I'm coming!' She raised her eyebrows at Meirian. 'Wish me luck — only last week, the Hardwicks' carriage got bogged down on the coast road, and they were stranded for hours — '

'*Isabelle!*'

Meirian laughed, going to the oak door to wave them off. When she had a quiet moment to herself, she opened Lyall's letter. It was brimming with exuberance, joy, hope and excitement and filled with vivid, detailed descriptions of the art gallery and preparations for the exhibition next month. However, the final few lines took her by surprise:

'I miss you terribly, Meirian! Everything here is wonderful and far exceeds expectations, but my dearest wish is that you were here to share it all with me.'

★　★　★

'It isn't like Mr Legh to miss church, is it, miss?' Mally said after Sunday service ended at St Radegund's. 'I wanted to thank him for them reading books. I hope he's all right.' She turned, grabbing little Norah's hand before the child could clamber up into the font. 'Mr Legh . . . Well, he *drinks*, dun't he, miss? Maybe he's had a skinful like Dad used to and he's sleeping it off.'

'I'm sure that's not the case, Mally,' replied Meirian, fervently hoping it wasn't. 'When I next see Mr Legh, I'll give him your thanks and tell him you're enjoying the books.'

They left the church, Mally presently running off ahead to join her mother. It was a bright, crisp morning, and Meirian and James slowed their pace along the beech avenue, falling behind the rest of the party returning to the manor house.

'Mally has a point about Mr Legh,' remarked Meirian thoughtfully.

'That he might've had a skinful and be sleeping it off?'

She cast him a withering glance. 'Mr Legh never misses church, James. Suppose he *is* ill? Now I think of it, he looked very pale when I saw him last.'

'George always looks like death warmed up.'

'For somebody who's supposed to be his friend, you're not very concerned!'

'He missed church, Meirian. It's not a crime, although I daresay Reverend Sutcliffe would have it a capital offence if he could,' said James, adding seriously, 'It was about this time of year

Eunice left him. Could be George just needs some privacy.'

That afternoon, Meirian finished a letter to Lyall and was sealing it when Annie came into her room with clean towels. 'Shall I give that to Alf for the post, miss?'

'Yes, thank — no, come to think of it. It's Sunday, so Alf and Gladys will want to be going over to visit her parents. I'll take it myself.'

After leaving her letter at The Swan, Meirian took the wagon up alongside the schoolhouse lodgings and knocked quietly. There was no response. Stepping back, she glanced at the small window of George Legh's room. Despite the hour, the curtain was still tightly closed. Meirian's concern increased. Nobody at The Swan, where the schoolmaster did much of his drinking, recalled seeing him since Friday. Suppose his grief at losing Eunice had become an unbearable burden? He'd looked particularly frail when Meirian last saw him. Suppose —

There was a crash. At that same instant, Meirian saw the flash of flames illuminating the room beyond the curtain. Tipping the latch, she burst inside. Tongues of fire were licking along a trail of spilled lamp oil. The lamp was smashed and aflame upon the wooden floor, and alongside it George Legh lay crumpled and still.

Catching up the rag rug from the hearth, Meirian swiftly crushed the rapidly spreading trail of fire. It was all over in a minute, but as she straightened, she was trembling and her heart thumping. She went to George Legh and gently turned him over. At least the flames had not reached him. His eyes were closed, his thin face bloodless. He was barely alive.

The lodgings consisted of a single room, and using all her strength, Meirian hauled the incumbent man up onto his bed, bundling the covers close about him before going with all speed through the dark village to fetch Henry Poulsom.

'George owes you his life, Meirian,' commented Henry later, snapping shut his bag. 'If he'd been left much longer, he wouldn't have needed a physician — it'd be work for the coffinmaker.'

'He *will* recover, though?' she murmured, her gaze never leaving the waxen face resting upon the hard calico pillow.

'Given time, and rest and care. I'll find one of the local women to sit with him tonight. Then you can be on your way — you look all in!'

'I'm all right, and *I'll* stay with Mr Legh,' she insisted softly. 'It's not — not right . . . he's no one of his own to watch with him while he's so ill.'

'You're a kind-hearted girl, Meirian.' He patted her shoulder. 'I'm afraid you're in for a long, difficult night. The illness has taken a particularly pernicious grip, because George is run down and his resistance is low. He'll likely be slipping in and out of consciousness.

There'll be deliriums, feverish fits. Can I at least fetch one of the women to sit with you?'

'I'll be fine alone, but can you please get word to Blackthorn? I don't want Haffie worrying where I am.'

'Glad to.' He put on his thick coat and hat. 'I'll come by first thing in the morning. If George takes a turn for the worse, knock up the stable lad at The Swan and tell him to run for me.'

It was a difficult night, as Henry Poulsom predicted. The hours seemed to crawl, and more than once, Meirian was upon the brink of running to The Swan for help. Mercifully, as dawn was breaking, George Legh's breathing steadied and his eyes flickered. Meirian watched him struggling to focus upon her face.

'Eunice?' he muttered thickly. 'Eunice, is — '

'It's me, Mr Legh, Meirian Penlan,' she whispered, soothing his moist forehead with a cool damp cloth. 'You're ill, but Dr Poulsom says you'll be well again soon.'

'The school . . . ' He shifted restlessly, his eyes dazed. 'I — I must — '

'You must rest.' She eased him back onto the pillows and poured a tumbler of the medicine. 'Sip this slowly. In a little while, you may have some custard. Sleep easy now, Mr Legh. Don't concern yourself with anything but getting better.'

His heavy-lidded eyes closed, as though even that small effort had exhausted his energy. When he'd drifted into a deep peaceful sleep, Meirian quickly tidied up after the night, and was about to prepare his custard only to discover the schoolmaster's cupboard was all but empty. Did the man never eat?

Preoccupied with her thoughts, she scarce noticed curious glances as she emerged from the schoolhouse, nor the coolness of the shopkeeper, and that folk abruptly stopped talking when she entered the bakery. It wasn't until she was scurrying back with her purchases that she suddenly became aware her appearance must be unkempt and dishevelled. She hadn't so much as washed her face or brushed her hair today! No wonder folk were staring. Then she spotted the wagon tucked under the trees alongside the school-house and realised with a jolt that it wasn't her untidy appearance that was causing the stir!

Flummoxed, she made a beeline across the green, only to come to face to face with Tod Weir conversing with a knot of people clustered about the old stocks.

'Good morning to you, Miss Penlan! Sure'n you're making an early start with Mr Legh,' he called. 'Or was it perhaps another late night for the pair of you?'

'That's no way to speak to a lady!'

James! Even as Meirian was spinning around, she heard Tod Weir fall. When she looked, he was sprawled across the ground, rubbing his jaw with the heel of his hand. Scrambling to his feet, Weir faced James squarely. Meirian's throat constricted. The bailiff's narrowed eyes blazed with fury, his fists clenched tightly at his sides. Meirian watched in horror, powerless to stop what was about to happen. Weir was by far the more powerful, stockier man; but inexplicably, James took the upper hand.

'I'd say you owe Miss Penlan an apology.'

The moment froze, Meirian certain Tod Weir would lash out. His florid features contorted, his gaze darting to the little crowd of curious onlookers. Somehow he gained control of his temper. 'My humblest apologies, Miss Penlan,' he declared without so much as a glance in her direction. 'My observation was surely mistaken.'

'Not merely mistaken, Weir,' remarked Henry Poulsom, sauntering into the fray and speaking so all those gathered might clearly hear. 'Utterly ignorant of the facts! George Legh was taken ill near to death. Miss Penlan stayed to nurse him at my bidding. Likely saved the man's life in the process. And *that* is surely a deed worth gossiping about, wouldn't you say?' he concluded, turning from the bailiff to Meirian. 'Miss Penlan, would you be kind enough to return to the schoolhouse with me and acquaint me with my patient's progress?'

Meirian fell into step beside the elderly man, and James did likewise.

'You shouldn't have hit him!' she muttered as they walked. 'I didn't even know you were in the village.'

'I came to visit George and bring Annie to take over nursing him so you can get some rest,' he answered tersely. 'Besides, Weir had it coming!'

'Undoubtedly,' remarked Henry as the three entered the schoolhouse. 'However, Meirian is quite right. You shouldn't have hit him. Tod Weir is a dangerous man to cross, and he won't relish being humiliated before the entire village. From now on, you'll have to watch your back, Jamie-boy!'

'Ohh, it's so romantic, miss! The squire fighting for your honour,' sighed Gladys dreamily while the two women were sitting in the drawing-room cutting strips of coloured paper and twisting and looping them into garlands for the Great Hall. 'It's like them tales from the olden days, when gentlemen fought duels for their lady's favours.'

'It was nothing of the sort. It's over and done, and the least said the sooner it'll be forgotten,' returned Meirian severely. 'What matters is that Mr Legh is at last on the mend, and with good food and plenty of rest up here at the manor house, should make a full recovery.'

'He's starting to look better. I reckon being out of bed has cheered him up too, even if he does have to stay upstairs until he's stronger,' considered Gladys, weaving red ribbon through green paper in a heart basket. 'He'd let himself go, hadn't he? And drunk himself soft after Eunice left him. Nothing to live for, being all on his own like that.'

'Well he's not all alone now, Gladys,' she replied crisply. 'Nor shall he be. Would you pass me the glue, please?'

'Here y'are, miss.' She sat back on her heels, ruminating upon the paper chains strewn all about her. 'I wonder would Alf pine if I left him? Or if he'd fight for *my* honour . . .'

With an irritated shake of her head, Meirian busied herself cutting, folding and pasting. The two women worked on without talking, each caught up in her thoughts, until Isabelle Caunce popped her head around the door.

'Henry and I are going to Kirkgate for Christmas shopping,' she beamed, surveying the festive sight before her. 'Do you want anything fetching from the shops, Meirian? We'll be off, then. You're both doing wonders with the garlands. The Great Hall will look absolutely splendid this year!'

Gladys waited until the door closed

before muttering, 'About time, too! I've heard there used to be high old times here, and the old squire was the life and soul of the party, but I never saw none of it! All the years I was here, Donald Caunce was mean and bad-tempered and forever picking fault. Made your life a right misery, he did. At least he never tried any funny business with me, although there's plenty of girls he more than tried with — *if* you take my meaning, miss.'

'Gladys, you shouldn't speak of such things!'

'Them days are gone, and good riddance, miss,' she said blithely, taking up huge handfuls of paper snowflakes and showering them over herself and Meirian. 'We're set for a right merry Christmas this year, and no mistake!'

★   ★   ★

Since George Legh still wasn't able to get downstairs, James and Meirian took a tray of tea up to his room to sit awhile and talk to him. He was swathed in blankets in the big chair beside the window, and a table groaning with books chosen by Isabelle from the library stood within his reach. He sipped his tea, holding the cup as though it were a great weight between hands that trembled slightly.

'It's most kind of you to invite me,' he murmured. 'However, I couldn't possibly impose; and besides, I'm much recovered and intend being back home by Christmas.'

'You'll do no such thing!' Meirian insisted. 'And you won't be imposing — Mrs Caunce would be deeply offended to imagine you believed that! You're very welcome to share our Christmas, and we'll all be delighted at your company.'

'Miss Penlan, really I — '

'Save your breath, George,' commented James. 'If Ma and Meirian have decided you're staying for Christmas, just give in gracefully and start making paper chains and heart baskets.'

George Legh looked from one to the other and his gaunt face relaxed into a genuine smile. 'Thank you. Actually, I used to be rather skilful at paper-folding when I was a boy.'

'That's settled, then,' said Meirian with a satisfied nod. 'I've closed the school until further notice, by the way.'

He nodded ruefully, adding, 'I only hope I shall be fit enough to go to church on Christmas Eve.'

'We'll see what Dr Poulsom says,' replied Meirian, gathering the tea things. 'If you're unable to go to St Radegund's yourself, I'm sure Reverend Sutcliffe will come and pray with you here.'

'Steady on, Meirian!' exclaimed James, aghast. 'This man's been ill — a visit from Reverend Sutcliffe will set him back months!'

'I'll leave you two to your gossip,' she responded, flouncing from the room with the tray. 'And James, I'll be in the Great Hall preparing for Yule, if you want to help.'

Alf and Becky had already brought long boards and trestles into the Great Hall and set them the length of the wall opposite the enormous fireplace. Annie and Mally were finishing scrubbing the worn stone floor when Meirian came in with the herb basket, ready to strew the damp floor with sweet-smelling rosemary.

'I'll give you a hand with that, miss.'

'No need, thanks, Annie,' she said with a smile. 'But Haffie's just making a brew, and Mally, I think she'll need a hand making the St Nicholas cake later.'

'I'll go and ask her,' said Mally with a grin, dashing off with the pail and brush. 'She let me bake a pie yesterday!'

'Miss Rees said my Mally could be a proper cook when she's older,' Annie related proudly. 'Said she has the patience and the light touch for it.'

'I'm sure Haffie's right, Annie. Mally's a clever and willing girl. She'll do well at whatever she sets her mind to,' replied Meirian, adding quietly,

'Have you any news?'

'Of Billy?' She shook her head vehemently. 'Nor do I want it. He stole what little we had. Walked out and left his own bairns penniless. I'll never forgive him for that!'

Meirian was alone in the Great Hall. Fingers of cold winter sun were reaching through the old glass and glowing upon the glossy holly leaves and shiny scarlet berries she was arranging around the fireplace.

James joined her, taking the boughs from her arms. 'Here, let me do that; I've a longer reach. Doesn't the rosemary smell nice?'

'Mmm.' She moved across the herb-strewn flags, crushing the stems beneath her feet and releasing even more of their fragrance. 'Becky's gathered a wonderful collection of evergreens — I've never seen so many different kinds.'

'Becky knows the Blackthorn woods better than anybody,' James said, securing the holly above the fire. 'He knows where everything grows and where everything lives. How does that look?'

She considered the swags of holly, woven through with dark green and golden ivy. 'A little higher on the right. Yes, that's better!'

She resumed sorting the swathes of bay, laurel, ivy, hollies, yew, pine boughs and cones into arrangements for decking the tables, walls, window ledges and candle branches.

'I heard from Lyall again today,' remarked James, taking an armful of pine and footing the ladder up to the roof beams. 'He seems brimful of confidence and taking all the fuss and faff in his stride.'

'I'd be a bundle of nerves in his place, but Lyall is very ... ebullient about the whole affair.'

'I thought that. And it isn't like him, Meirian.' James frowned, pausing from festooning the ancient beams. 'Lyall's always been quiet, unassuming. Riven with doubts and anxieties. He's been through a really bad patch lately, too.'

'I know,' she murmured, aware of his keen glance and adding, 'Lyall told me how he found your father, and about the memories and the dreams troubling him.'

'It was a nasty business. It hit Lyall hard. Ma, too.' He sighed in regret. 'I should've been here.'

'You must've missed your family and home very much when you were in the army.'

'I didn't leave Blackthorn because I wanted to go away, Meirian,' he confessed bleakly. 'I went because I couldn't honourably remain here — my late father saw to that!'

★　★　★

It was Blackthorn tradition that everybody on the estate finish work early on the day of Yule. From dusk onwards, folk began wending their ways up towards the ancient manor house to celebrate looking forward to the end of winter and the coming of spring. Warm light spilled from the windows of the Great Hall and lively music drifted on the cold, icy air as neighbours and old friends were welcomed at the oak front door by James and Meirian before pouring inside to join the feast.

'Isn't this wonderful!' enthused Isabelle when the festivities were in full swing. 'This is how Yuletide *should* be celebrated.'

'It's a shame you'll not be with us for Christmas, Henry,' said James, refilling the doctor's glass. 'We had some grand times when you used to spend the festive season here with us.'

'Happy days indeed!' he agreed amiably. 'But I'll be going up to Carlisle as usual — Christmas wouldn't be Christmas without Rosamund and Jonathan and little Daisy.'

'When do you leave, Dr Poulsom?'

'Can't wait to get rid of me, eh?' He beamed at Meirian over the rims of his spectacles. 'I set off the day after tomorrow and arrive Christmas Eve

— icy roads and freezing weather not withstanding.'

'We'll have to make the most of you while you're still here with us,' said Isabelle with a smile, taking his arm and leading him towards the centre of the hall where dancers were whirling to a rousing reel. 'I do believe Becky is playing our tune.'

'That's the last we'll see of them for a while.' James grinned down at Meirian. 'You know, I reckon everyone who's coming is already here. We've greeted them and wished them well . . . I think we can relax and start enjoying ourselves now. Lambswool?'

'I'm sure it's highly intoxicating,' she commented as he led her towards a gaily decked table set with fruit, nuts, sweetmeats and biscuits. In the centre stood a huge silver dish brimming with a heady, fragrant concoction of spiced ale and apples. 'However, I'll try it — just a sample, mind!'

'You can pour me one while you're at it,' Becky Beswick said as he approached, pocketing his precious flute.

'Taking a well-earned break from playing for us, Becky?' said Meirian, gasping slightly at the potency of the lambswool. 'The music is wonderful! I've never heard such invigorating tunes.'

'Made for dancing, they be.' He nodded, accepting the cup James proffered. 'You've not forgotten you owe me a jug of The Swan's best grog, have you? A few weeks back, I told you the river'd freeze afore Christmas and you bet me it wouldn't. It's been froze solid as a rock these past two days!'

'Becky's right,' chipped in Meirian blithely, sipping her lambswool. 'All the village children have been skating and sledging on it. Frozen solid, exactly as Becky says.'

'I hadn't noticed,' grumbled James, reaching behind the settle where he'd hidden a flask of dark Jamaican rum. 'You'll have to make do with this till

I see you at The Swan. You may take this pouch of baccy, as well. Merry Christmas.'

'And you!' retorted Becky, shaking James's hand. 'Thank'ee.'

'The river's frozen hard as iron,' mused Meirian. 'Why isn't Swallowhole Mere frozen too?'

'The devil's hot breath comes up from under the mere bed so the watter never freezes.' With that, Becky drained his cup, took up his flute, and disappeared into the throng of dancing to rejoin the musicians.

James watched him go, glancing around the heaving crowd of happy folk, their merry-making, laughter and tapping feet ringing up and around the ancient rafters of the Great Hall. He leaned close to Meirian's ear to be heard. 'No one's going to miss us if we slip away. Fetch your warmest coat, your hat and your gloves.'

'Where are we going?' she protested. 'What about the Yule?'

'Have you ever done any skating?

Well the river's frozen, so now's your chance!'

In no time at all, they were hurrying across the slippery grass and through the orchard down to the riverbank. The night was perfectly still. The rushing waters of the river were frozen into silence; a glistening white ribbon winding away beneath the luminous, frosty moon.

'You had this planned all along, didn't you?' sighed Meirian happily when they were seated upon the fallen bole and James was showing her how to strap on the heavy wooden skates. 'Doesn't everywhere look beautiful? It's as bright as day!'

'It'll get brighter yet,' he replied, gazing at the velvety ink-blue sky scattered with hundreds of sparkling stars. 'But aren't the stars resplendent tonight.'

Meirian raised her face to look and nodded wordlessly. She'd never before seen a night sky so blue, or stars so radiant, or the moon so incredibly silvery. Once on the frozen river, she slipped and slithered, trying to steady her balance while James held her upright.

'Keep your knees soft like they're springs, and lean forward a little. Keep your free arm outstretched to help your balance,' he instructed. 'You won't fall.'

'Are you sure of that?' she gasped, feeling her feet go from under her yet still remaining standing.

'It's a promise.' He was holding her securely, taking her weight as they began gliding slowly forwards. 'Instead of putting one foot before the other, try swaying from side to side — that's the way! We'll get to Kirkgate in no time!'

'Kirkgate?' she spluttered. 'That's *miles* away!'

'By road, aye. As the crow flies and the river bends, however, it's not so very far,' he replied, a smile lighting his blue eyes. 'Don't worry, we needn't skate all the way to Kirkgate.'

But they did! Meirian felt completely safe with James's arm about her and his hand holding hers. Once she found the rhythm of gliding from side to side, she revelled in every minute of their skating through the moonlit meadows and woodland.

'That's Kirkgate Castle up ahead,' James pointed out when they'd paused for a breather. The twelfth-century castle loomed formidable and majestic, its ruined towers and battlements silhouetted against the starry winter sky and washed with moonlight.

'Are they torches?' queried Meirian as they skated on and distant plumes of flames spitting and spluttering into the icy air slid into view below the castle walls. 'Oh look, lots of folk are skating in the torchlight!'

'Kirkgate's a busy little town. It's a big occasion when the river freezes. They put on an ice fair.'

Carollers were on the ice singing for coins in the pools of torchlight beneath the castle; stalls were dotted along the edges of the frozen river selling chocolate, savoury pies, candies and currant buns; and a colourfully dressed man was skating back and forth offering roasted chestnuts and split potatoes. James purchased two bags of chestnuts and some hot chocolate and they sat on the riverbank, their backs comfortably against the castle walls, as they ate and drank and watched the skaters skimming across the moonlit river.

'We can hire a chaise, if you like?' suggested James. 'And drive home.'

'I wouldn't hear of it!' laughed Meirian, already scrambling down onto the ice. 'I want to skate!'

Gliding hand in hand through the cold starry night, it seemed no time at all before the manor house came into sight once more. After changing into their shoes at the fallen bole, James put his arm about Meirian's waist and they wandered back through the icy orchard, pausing at a mature apple tree still bearing a scattering of tiny yellow fruits that glowed in the moonshine like golden lamps.

'Did you know mistletoe likes growing on old apple trees?' he asked, drawing her beneath the berry-laden boughs and touching his lips to hers. Responding instinctively, Meirian moved closer into his arms as their kiss deepened.

Just then, revellers exploded from the Great Hall and came careening down the garden, singing and laughing and shaking bell-sticks.

'Perhaps they'll go away!' James whispered against Meirian's ear.

They didn't. Every one of them came piling into the orchard, waving their bell-sticks. James and Meirian slipped away unseen between the trees as the merry-makers encircled one of the fruit trees and began dancing, rattling their bell-sticks and chanting loudly.

Arms entwined, James and Meirian strolled away up the garden towards the manor house. 'Aren't you going to ask me what they're doing?'

Meirian gazed up at him and shook her head, her eyes shining. They laughed softly, their faces close as they reached the oaken door and returned to the Yule celebrations.

Becky and the musicians were playing 'I Saw Three Ships'; some folk were singing along while many more were stepping out in a long chain, weaving under and through in the intricate patterns of an old Lancashire round dance. Somebody grabbed James as they passed him by and he turned, holding out his hand to Meirian. Smiling, she shook her head and backed away even as James was dragged into the boisterous sea of dancers.

Meirian found a quiet corner, half-hidden from view by the screen's carved trusses, and was content to sit and watch and relive the evening she'd spent with James, and those few breathless moments beneath the mistletoe in the icy apple orchard.

Upon the clock of St Ragegund's striking midnight, the squire and his family traditionally withdrew from the Yule celebrations and quit the Great

Hall amid rousing cheers as founders of the feast, leaving the merry-makers to continue their revels through the night.

'Must be getting old,' commented Henry, sinking into an armchair in the drawing-room. 'I'm all worn out and ready for my bed.'

'Wasn't it a splendid night, though!' exclaimed Isabelle with satisfaction. 'Did you enjoy it, Meirian?'

'I had the most wonderful night,' she murmured, her eyes still alight. 'Oh, and the Great Hall looks absolutely beautiful!'

James fleetingly caught Meirian's eye. 'I'll always remember tonight.'

'Everyone will, for years to come,' agreed Henry, beaming across at Isabelle. 'You've given us — ah, here's Hafwen with the tea. Oatcakes, too!'

'Aye, you'll need some good plain sustenance after all that rich food and frolicking,' replied Hafwen, setting down the tray. 'Here's the evening post. There's a letter for you, Dr Poulsom. The lad knew you'd be up here, so he brought it with ours.'

'It's from Rosamund! I hope nothing's wrong.' Henry frowned, glancing at the elegant handwriting before breaking the seal and unfolding the page. 'Well, I'll be!' His kindly face broke into the widest smile. 'They're travelling down from Carlisle, Isabelle — Rosamund and her family are coming home for Christmas!'

⋆ ⋆ ⋆

Although it had been a long and eventful day, Meirian couldn't sleep. Hours after the festivities in the Great Hall had finally drawn to a close and the last of the village folk wandered homewards, she lay wide awake thinking of James and savouring the warm happiness enveloping her upon that longest night of the year.

Presently, she rose and padded downstairs. It was still very early. Gladys and Annie wouldn't be up for ages yet so Meirian expected to find the kitchen deserted, and was surprised to find a candle burning and Haffie in her rocking chair beside the fire, an open book across her lap as she dozed.

'Hello, lovey.' The housekeeper stirred at Meirian's approach. 'Fancy some cocoa? It'll still be hot.'

'Grand!' replied Meirian, helping herself from the pot. 'I thought you'd have been abed hours ago. You never stopped working yesterday.'

'Oh, it wasn't too bad. Having Annie and Mally — young Joe, too — makes a big difference,' said Hafwen, thinking aloud. 'We'll need them, what with George Legh being here, all the missus's plans for the festive season, and now four more company.'

'Four more company?'

'Miss Rosamund and her family, and Dr Poulsom. The missus has invited them to stay over Christmas,' went on Hafwen, adding with a knowing nod, 'Rosamund home for Christmas? Now *there's* a curious to-do.'

'Why?' yawned Meirian, drinking her

cocoa. 'What's curious about a daughter visiting her father at Christmas?'

'If you'd been here when they were all youngsters, it'd be plain as a pikestaff,' answered Hafwen, warming to the subject. 'Rosamund, James and Lyall were best friends. James was oldest, and Rosamund was about the same age as Lyall, who even as a little lad worshipped the ground she walked on. 'Course, she never noticed him. Rosamund only had eyes for James!'

Now Hafwen had Meirian's full attention. 'Rosamund and James were childhood sweethearts?'

'Everyone expected them to wed when she was old enough. But then . . . ' The housekeeper dropped her voice. ' . . . James upped and left Blackthorn without a word. Next thing, Rosamund's gone too. Off up north to stay with her late mother's sister in Carlisle. She married Jonathan Petherbridge, who's years older than her, and had a little girl. But she's never shown her face here since the day she left Blackthorn when she was fifteen.'

'I don't understand what point you're making, Haffie,' said Meirian briskly. 'Why *shouldn't* she come home?'

'Why now, that's the question. Mark my words, Meirian, it's far more than coincidence that the first Christmastide James is back here at the manor house is the first occasion Rosamund Poulsom chooses to spend Christmas in Blackthorn!'

10

'Stand up on here, lovey,' said Hafwen, dragging the dolly-stool alongside the kitchen table. 'Now you'll be able to give the bowl a good stir. Make sure all the candied peel and sultanas are well mixed in, that's the way.'

'Shall I put the marmalade in now, Aunt Hafwen? And this stuff?' Daisy carefully picked up the tumbler of malt whiskey and sniffed it gingerly. 'Oh! It's *horrible*!'

'Aye, well your grandad likes it in his bun loaf,' replied Hafwen, greasing tins and glancing to the far end of the table where Meirian and the child's mother were working side by side. 'We're baking this specially for him because he's spending Christmas with us. Once you've done that, you can cut out the gingerbread men and put on their faces — that's if your mam and Meirian stop chattering long enough to get the dough made and rolled out.'

'Why is Grandpa's cake called a bun loaf, Aunt Hafwen?' asked Daisy, spooning glistening marmalade into the mixture. 'It's a funny name, isn't it? It doesn't look like a bun, so why is it called a *bun* loaf?'

'Well . . . erm,' floundered Hafwen, meeting Daisy's bright, blue inquisitive eyes. 'Tell you what, shall we bake something nice for your pa's tea next?'

'Papa would like that. He likes things with almonds in them,' said Daisy, scraping the mixture into the tin. 'Why *is* it called a bun loaf, Aunt Hafwen? We didn't put any buns in it, did we?'

'No, we didn't. Why don't we ask Grandpa later, eh? I bet he'll know. While I put the bun loaf to bake, will you start putting the dirty dishes into the sink ready for Annie to wash . . . ?'

Rosamund Petherbridge's gaze rested upon her little daughter as she bustled to and from the big brown sink, and she sighed contentedly. 'It's wonderful to be at Blackthorn again, Meirian! It brings back so many happy memories of when Mama was alive and we were all together.'

'You've been away a long time, I believe,' Meirian remarked, passing the rolling pin. 'Why didn't you come home sooner?'

'Oh, all sorts of reasons. It would've been difficult before,' she answered vaguely, going on, 'I'm really glad we're here now, though. I can remember so many lovely Christmasses! Mama and Aunt Isabelle and Hafwen and me here in the kitchen making the cakes and biscuits and puddings, and now I'm home again and doing those things with my own daughter.'

'Daisy's a lovely child.' Meirian smiled. It was impossible not to warm to the golden-curled little girl with her shy ways and boundless curiosity about anything and everything. However, for no logical reason, Meirian had not expected to like Rosamund Pether-bridge — but found she did. 'You must be very proud of her.'

Rosamund laughed softly, placing a batch of rolled dough ready for Daisy to cut into gingerbread men. 'I was so scared when I discovered I was with child, Meirian! I was still very young, and . . . But, I need not have worried. Marrying Jonathan and having Daisy are the most wonderfully happy things that could ever have happened to me. Jonathan and I would dearly love another child,' she confided in a low voice. 'Sadly, we haven't yet been blessed.'

Leaving Daisy with the gingerbread men, the two women tidied away the treacle and flour pots before going to the sink and washing their sticky hands. Beyond the window, they could see James, Becky and Alf trekking back and forth from the river and down into the wood hauling a sledge loaded with blocks of ice.

'I've done the faces,' said Daisy, squeezing between them to see what her mama and Meirian were looking at.

'What are they doing? What's that on the sledge?'

'It's ice,' replied Meirian, lifting Daisy up so she could better see from the window. 'The river's frozen, so the men are cutting big pieces of ice and taking it to the ice-house.'

'Why?' asked Daisy, raising her chubby face and huge blue eyes to Meirian. 'What's an ice-house?'

'Hafwen needs lots of ice to make jellies and mousses,' explained Meirian with a smile. 'The men store the ice in a special, very cold little house buried underground in the woods. It stays frozen there for months and months and months.'

Daisy's eyes widened, and she looked to Rosamund. 'May I go to see the cold little house? May I, Mama?'

'I suppose so — but you'll need to put on your boots and coat and hat first.'

'Tea's up for them as wants it,' announced Hafwen. 'There's tea and snap for them outside, too.'

'I'll take it out, Haffie,' said Meirian, fetching her shawl and glancing to Rosamund. 'Would you like me to take Daisy with me?'

'If you're sure it won't be any bother?'

'No bother at all — come on, Daisy!'

Carrying the tea and snap-basket over one arm and taking hold of Daisy's tiny gloved hand, Meirian set off across the garden to meet the men in the wood.

'Tea's up! Hot pasties, too,' she announced, setting the basket onto a stump so the men might help themselves. 'Daisy's come to see the ice-house.'

'Queer little place it is, Daisy,' said James, dipping into the basket and offering her a pasty before sharing the others out to Becky and Alf and helping himself. 'Why don't you sit here with us, and I'll tell you about the family of white bears — *white* bears, mark you, not ordinary black or brown bears — of white bears who lived in the ice-house when I was your age . . . '

With a backward glance at Daisy, sitting cross-legged nibbling her pasty and gazing wide-eyed up at James, Meirian hurried back through the woods to the manor house. They were putting away the crockery when the passage door swung open and Lyall strode into the kitchen, his face animated and wreathed in smiles.

'Rosamund! I could hardly believe it when I heard you'd be home for Christmas!' he exclaimed, wrapping her in a fierce hug before holding her at arm's length. 'Oh, it's so good to see you again.'

'Lyall,' she murmured, her hand gently touching his cheek. 'You're all grown up!'

'We both are, I suppose!'

'Not so anybody'd notice,' grumbled Hafwen, shooing them away from where she was putting away the baking tins. 'The pair of you, in here and under my feet like always! Mind, I'm glad to see you safe and sound, Mr Lyall.

Becky was telling me the roads from Preston are bad and getting worse.'

'Becky's absolutely right, as always. It was a pretty hazardous journey, but I had to get here.' He grinned, still holding Rosamund's hands within his own. 'Napoleon's army couldn't have kept me from Blackthorn this Christmas!'

'How was your trip to Preston — nasty, grimy place that it is?'

'Perfect, Hafwen, except for the food. It wasn't a patch on your cooking.' He beamed across at her. 'I'm returning next week to put the finishing touches to the exhibition, and I'll be staying with the Mathers until it's over. How long are you staying at Blackthorn, Rosamund? Months, I hope!'

'Sadly, only until after Christmastide.' She laughed. 'Then we'll need to go home. Jonathan and his juniors are preparing an important case that's coming to trial shortly. What with one thing and another, he's very busy at present.'

'Henry was saying Jonathan is to be made a judge,' said Lyall, adding, 'I saw him when I came in. He and George are talking books in the drawing-room, but where's your little girl? I can't wait to meet her!'

'She's out there,' said Rosamund with a smile, glancing from the window to where the little procession was on its way down to the river. Daisy was seated atop the empty sledge chattering nineteen to the dozen to James as he pushed the sledge on its broad wheels across the hard white ground.

'Meirian said James was telling Daisy about the white bears earlier.'

'Not the white bears,' guffawed Lyall. 'I recall him telling *us* about the white bears when we were small. I was twenty before I realised it was a fairy story.'

Rosamund chuckled as they moved from the window, remembering. 'What about the tale he told us on Hermitage Island that Easter we were . . . '

Meirian didn't hear the rest of their reminiscences. She tarried in the kitchen, waiting until Lyall and Rosamund's voices faded along the passageway. For the first time since arriving at Blackthorn, she felt an outsider. With a heavy sigh, she continued to watch from the window until James and little Daisy disappeared from her sight down towards the frozen river.

*   *   *

Meirian was slithering across the icy cobbles clutching her sewing bag when Lyall came storming out from the woods, hailing her abruptly. 'Have you seen Tod Weir?'

'He's still in Liverpool,' she said.

'Damn the man!' he muttered, agitatedly raking a hand through his dark hair. 'When's he expected back?'

'Some time today, I believe,' she replied, suddenly realising Lyall had come from the direction of the bailiff's cottage and recalling the peculiar argument between the two men she'd witnessed from the squint. Her mouth compressed with disapproval. 'Apart from Blackthorn business in the town, I suspect Tod Weir has dealings of his own making in Liverpool!'

'He's certainly not without means,' Lyall said bitterly, turning on his heel and making for the house, 'thanks to my father's bounty!'

With an exasperated shake of her head, Meirian hurried into the barn, where James was shaping a piece of smooth wood on the workbench. He looked up and smiled when she entered. 'Have you found anything suitable?'

'I think so.' Opening the sewing bag, Meirian brought out scraps of velvet, ribbons and a selection of bright little buttons. 'How about the deep green velvet for the saddle? I'll pad it well. And red ribbons for the harness and reins? I can trim them all with these pearly buttons. If you like the idea, that is.'

'Sounds grand.' He grinned, standing back and considering the horse emerging from the wood he was working.

'Couldn't do this without your help.'

'I'll comb out some wool for the mane and tail,' went on Meirian, running her fingers over the little wooden horse. 'Daisy is going to love this!'

'It's nothing fancy, but I checked with Jonathan that she doesn't have a hobby horse, so this'll be something to remember us by.'

'Daisy could never forget you,' murmured Meirian, wistfully watching him making the Christmas gift for Rosamund's daughter. 'I'd best take some measurements and get started on the saddle — it'll be Christmas before we know it!'

*   *   *

'Thanks for coming with me,' Lyall said, offering his hand to help Meirian from the sculler and ashore onto Hermitage Island. 'I'm sure I'm taking you away from your work.'

'Not at all. I had sewing, but I've

finished it,' she replied, loath to admit even to herself that she'd been glad to escape the manor house and the unwelcome direction of her thoughts whenever she saw James and Rosamund Petherbridge exchanging a word or a smile. 'Besides, now you've decided to clear up your father's belongings, it's best not to dilly-dally.'

'I couldn't have faced it before,' he confided, showing her into the lodge. 'But somehow now, I want to get it over and done before I go back to Preston and a New Year begins.'

Together they sorted, folded and packed Donald Caunce's clothing and personal effects ready for removal from the island. 'All my father's guns are to go, too,' said Lyall dismally when the afternoon was closing in and their task was all but done. 'Except those fancy silver duelling pistols in the alcove above the bureau. I — I always liked those when I was a boy. Pa used to say he'd give them to me when I was a man. I suppose he must've forgotten . . . '

Although he looked away from her, Meirian saw the sorrow and grief etched in his face, and her heart went out to him. 'The hour grows late, Lyall,' she said. 'You've done almost everything, and it doesn't need to be finished today. We'll come back first thing tomorrow.'

He shook his head stubbornly, staring into the alcove. 'The bureau's going to be the hardest of Pa's possessions to sort through, Meirian. All his personal things are in there. I must get it over with. Once it's done, I can put all this behind me and look to the future.'

'Are you all right?' she asked anxiously, moving to Lyall's side and realising how tired and emotional he was. 'We really should go home.'

'There's only his bureau to do now,' he mumbled, going into the alcove where a huge deeply upholstered chair stood before a formidable walnut bureau, the ornate silver duelling pistols displayed in pride of place above. 'Pa was very fond of this bureau, you know. It's been passed down from father to son for centuries. It used to be in the study at the manor house. When — when James and I were little, Pa used to bring us presents from his trips and hide them in the bureau's secret compartments.' He laughed shakily, opening the heavy polished lid. 'It'd take us ages to press the right springs and find our presents.'

'Whyever does it have secret compartments?' she asked, intrigued at the array of drawers, pigeonholes, shelves and cubbies within the lavishly carved writing desk.

'When the Caunces were recusants, and during the Jacobite Rebellion and the Civil War, all sorts of dangerous documents and messages were hidden in this bureau. Whenever the manor house was searched, nothing incriminating was ever discovered by the enemy because everything of importance to the family was kept safe and secret in the hidden compartments.'

'Ah, but did you and James find your boyhood presents?' she asked lightly, immensely pleased to see Lyall's melancholy lifting a little. 'There must be dozens of hiding places.'

'There are a fair few — but Pa showed us where all the hidden compartments are, and how to open them.' Lyall deftly touched his fingertips to carvings, beadings and corners within the bureau's various drawers, shelves and pigeonholes and one by one, secret enclosures were revealed as if by magic. 'You can imagine how exciting this was for two adventurous young boys! Unfortunately, these hiding places are all quite empty now, but in those days there would be sweets and toys and games — it was absolutely thrilling!'

'It must've been.' She smiled, watching Lyall run his fingers over the bottles of ink, pens, nibs, wafers and seals, for the briefest moment lost in memories of happier times. She glanced away, leaving him to his thoughts, and was gathering up the jumble of old newspapers, journals and gun catalogues heaped in the corner of the alcove when Lyall's sudden gasp of astonishment had her spinning around.

'Good Lord, Meirian.' He turned from the bureau to face her, his palm outstretched. 'The amethyst necklace!'

The ancient gems were gleaming and glowing in the firelight, reflecting a myriad of tiny flames in their liquid colour and old, mellow gold. Meirian could scarcely believe her eyes. 'Where was it?'

'Inside the lid of the writing slope,' he replied in wonder, unable to take his eyes from the jewels. 'I didn't even know there was a false panel there — I found it quite by chance!'

Meirian was on her feet, gazing from the necklace to the slope within the bureau. 'What else is in the compartment?'

'Just papers, I think.' He reached inside, withdrawing a small bundle and leafing through them. 'Letters to my father — oh, I shouldn't be reading these. They're . . . they're personal.' Hastily refolding the sheets, Lyall thrust them back into the compartment and closed the panel with a soft click. 'I — I'll burn them. Not today, though. I know we haven't quite finished, Meirian, but you were right; I've had enough. Shall we go home now?'

'Of course,' she replied, startled by Lyall's sudden change of mood. He was closing up the bureau, obviously struggling to regain his composure, and she could only wonder what was in those letters to disconcert him so.

★ ★ ★

On Christmas Eve night, Isabelle Caunce stood before the glass in her parlour and considered her reflection, touching the jewels about her throat with her fingertips. 'I never thought to see these again, Meirian,' she mused, meeting the younger woman's gaze through the mirror. 'Donald had taken them after all. I suspected he might've, but somehow kept hoping even he wasn't capable of such a despicable act. It isn't merely my necklace, you see. This is a family heirloom, to be passed on to the woman James marries, and to the wife their son chooses.'

'I wonder why he took it? The old squire, I mean,' mused Meirian, gazing at the exquisitely beautiful medieval necklace. 'It went missing long before he died, didn't it? He obviously hadn't sold it or given it away to — to — '

'One of his lady friends?' put in Isabelle wryly. 'No. Quite. So, why *did* Donald steal the necklace from my jewel casket and hide it away in a secret compartment in his bureau on Hermitage Island? We'll never know, Meirian,' she finished, glancing around at the tap upon the parlour door. '*That* particular secret died with him.'

'Ready, ladies?' Lyall was beaming as he put his head around the door. 'Everyone's downstairs and ready to set off.'

Lyall and Jonathan Petherbridge were helping George Legh through the oaken door and out into the carriage. The three men, together with Rosamund and Daisy, were to travel by carriage, while the rest of the family and household were to make the torchlit pilgrimage to St Radegund's along the beech avenue on foot.

There was a flurry of last-minute activity, and as Meirian was hurrying back to the kitchen in search of the stone pigs, she saw Rosamund crossing the cobbles to board the carriage and James striding after her.

'Rosie!' he hissed. 'I must see you!'

'No, James.'

'*Yes!*' he insisted, catching hold of her wrist and staying her from walking from him. 'Too much has been left unsaid between us — *please*, Rosie!'

'Very well.' She stepped free of his grasp. 'Tonight. After church.'

'I'll wait for you in the drawing-room,' he murmured quickly, as others were approaching. 'Come as soon as you're able!'

With a heavy heart, Meirian walked beside Hafwen along the beech avenue to St Radegund's. Seated in the family pew, the candles blurred in her eyes and she heard scarcely a word of the service. Home again and at last alone with her thoughts, she lay wakeful, listening to the now familiar creaks and sighs as the old timber house settled for the night.

Again and again, her imagination strayed to the drawing-room. Was James waiting there in the silence? Was Rosamund even now starting down the stairs to keep their assignation?

* * *

That Christmas was the most joyous the manor house had seen in many a year, with the whole family and others besides enveloped in the warmth of Blackthorn's hospitality.

'Henry has asked me to be his wife, Meirian,' revealed Isabelle Caunce when they were in her parlour answering the seasonal letters. 'You're the first I've told!'

'What wonderful news, ma'am! Mind, I can't say I'm surprised — the pair of you make a fine couple!'

'I love him dearly. Henry's a fine man, and we're the very best of friends.' Isabelle beamed, her face pink with happiness. 'We'll announce the news at breakfast on the morning Rosamund and Jonathan are leaving. Lyall's going back to Preston that day too, so it'll be the last occasion we're all together for a while.'

'When's the wedding to be?'

'Oh, we'll marry quietly by and by. Neither of us wants any fuss,' she replied. 'I want you to know that my marriage won't affect your position here, Meirian. Blackthorn is your home for as long as you wish. Besides, James couldn't be without you now!'

Isabelle Caunce's words lingered in Meirian's mind. If only James *did* want and need her! Instead, he was all too plainly rekindling the romance with his childhood sweetheart.

* * *

Daisy and Joe Wilcox were of an age and had become firm pals. The pair were racing round the drying green taking turns with the hobby horse while Annie pegged out the wash.

'Joe!' she called, a wooden peg between her teeth. 'Shouldn't you be doing your chores?'

'Leave them be, Annie,' put in James quietly, sauntering from the house. 'You're only young once, and it passes by quick enough.'

'It does that, sir.' She smiled up at him. 'Joe'll miss the little lass when she goes home. Tomorrow, in't it?'

He nodded. 'It's a shame Rosie and her family can't stay longer. The place will seem very empty without Daisy rushing about asking questions.'

'She *is* a curious one, sir. A right ray of sunshine, too!'

Meirian was taking a breath of air at the study window, lost in thought. She hadn't intended to eavesdrop, however the ache deep within her sharpened at hearing James speak of Rosamund and her daughter and how sorely he'd miss them both. When she stepped away from the window, James glimpsed the movement and waved to her.

'Meirian! I promised Rosie and Daisy a trip across to Hermitage Island,' he called, sprinting over to the window. 'Would you care to join us? Hafwen's packing a basket for a winter picnic. It's set fair to be a nice bright day.'

'Is Mr Petherbridge going, too?' she heard herself ask.

James shook his head. 'Jonathan and George are going to Kirkgate. There's a speaker they want to hear at the Institute. Lyall can't come, either. He's busy getting ready for Preston. So is it to be a picnic for four?'

Meirian compressed her lips. She knew James was only inviting her out of politeness. It was obvious he and

Rosamund wanted to spend their last afternoon alone together. 'No. I have work to finish.'

'That's a pity. I'll see you when we get back, then?'

A little later, she watched them setting off towards Swallowhole Mere. Talking and laughing, they each held one of Daisy's hands, swinging her up over the hummocky places on the rough path. Blinking back treacherous tears, Meirian returned to her desk and tried in vain to concentrate upon the household accounts.

* * *

The following morning, Henry and Isabelle announced their betrothal and were soundly congratulated and toasted around the breakfast table. Soon afterwards, Lyall said his farewells and made ready to set off. He looked pale and drawn, and Meirian was concerned. It was a long, arduous ride up to Preston, especially in the middle of winter. It seemed to her that Lyall hadn't been himself since they'd sorted and disposed of his dead father's belongings. It was an emotional ordeal she remembered well from her own experience, and had obviously taken its toll upon Lyall.

She followed him out to the stable-yard, and they were talking quietly when Tod Weir emerged from the ice-house and strode through the trees towards them. 'Good morning, Miss Penlan! And to you, Mr Lyall. I was hoping to see you before you depart.' He handed Lyall a package, and Meirian heard the younger man's sharp intake of breath. 'The liniment you asked for, sir. If the hoof starts to swell, apply it liberally.'

Lyall snatched the package, glowering at the bailiff, his dark eyes mutinous. 'Not before time, either!'

'Just as you say, sir.' Tod Weir tipped his hat in a mocking gesture. 'I'm sure you'll find it most effective for what ails.'

The instant Weir was out of earshot, Meirian turned to Lyall. 'Whatever was that all about?'

'Nothing.' He stowed the package deep into his saddlebag. 'Nothing at all.'

A little after midday, the rest of the family and servants gathered at the oaken door to bid farewell to the Petherbridges. They were about to leave when Daisy broke away from her mother's hand, scampering across the cobbles and flinging herself at James.

'Thank you for my hobby horse!' she cried, raising her huge blue eyes to his. 'I'll take very good care of him!'

'I know that,' laughed James, swinging her up into his arms and carrying her to Rosamund and Jonathan waiting at the carriage. 'Remember to ride him often, won't you?'

'Thank you for a lovely Christmas.' Jonathan Petherbridge extended his hand with a warm smile. 'Good-bye, James.'

'Be sure you visit again soon, Jonathan. All the best with the appointment. If there were more men with your principles on the bench, justice would more wisely and readily be done.' Turning to Rosamund, James merely smiled down at her, his words suddenly soft. 'Don't be a stranger to Blackthorn, Rosie.'

With the Petherbridges' carriage disappearing down the drive, everyone drifted indoors. Meirian was going along the passageway towards the kitchen with Gladys.

'They say it's a wise man knows his own bairn, but that little lass certainly knows her own daddy, dun't she?' Gladys said with a grin. 'Does Mr Petherbridge know though, that's the thing.'

'Does he know what?' retorted Meiran irritably.

'Surely you've noticed, miss! That lass is the living spit of James,' went on Gladys in astonishment. 'Daisy is Captain Caunce's daughter — I thought *everybody* knew that!'

11

'Are you sure about running the school until George is recovered?' queried James, coming into the study. 'I'd have thought you already had enough to do.'

'If I couldn't cope, I wouldn't have volunteered,' Meirian answered tartly, not looking up from the inventory she was checking. 'Mr Legh thought it a good idea, and it's only for a few weeks until Dr Poulsom says he can resume teaching.

'Have you any objections?'

'None.' He spread his hands, dropping into the winged chair. 'George certainly isn't strong enough yet. Besides, the longer he stays here, the longer he stays sober.'

'Mr Legh told me he's done with the drink for good,' she said quietly. 'I believe him.'

'Is that so — about George turning

teetotal, I mean? He's likely done it in the nick of time.' James paused, watching Meirian while she worked. 'Why didn't you tell me George had stopped drinking?'

'I haven't had the opportunity to tell you anything recently, have I?'

He frowned slightly before continuing, 'Do you recall Jonathan telling us about a play he and Rosamund recently saw in Carlisle? You said you'd like to see it. I read in the *Gazette* the players are bringing it to Kirkgate for a couple of performances. Would you like to go?'

'I don't believe so, thank you all the same.'

James leaned back in the winged chair, considering her for a long moment. 'What is it you're not saying, Meirian? You've something gnawing on your mind, and it isn't like you not to come straight out and tell me what it is. It's not your way to be sullen and brooding.'

'I'm amazed you've even noticed what my way is! You've been so preoccupied with — ' The bitter retort was uttered before Meirian could check her tongue. Her cheeks flamed and she lowered her eyes to her writing tablet. 'My apologies. I shouldn't have spoken out of turn.'

James's jaw set. He remained silent, only the sombre ticking of the tall clock breaking the increasing tension. 'You mean preoccupied with Rosie, don't you?' he said at length, his piercing blue eyes boring into her. 'Isn't *that* what you mean?'

Meirian tilted her chin and met his relentless gaze steadily. 'Yes, I suppose it is. After we . . . After that . . . ' For once, she failed to find words.

He expelled a deep sigh. 'Meirian, I have feelings for you. From your kiss that night in the orchard, I believe you have them for me, too. Rosie means a great deal to me. She always will.' He went on simply, 'It was grand seeing her again, seeing Daisy for the first time and meeting Jonathan, too. Rosie and I *did* spend a lot of time together, and

I'm sorry if you were offended, but I'm not my father, Meirian! I don't make a habit of deceiving women and ruining their lives. You either trust me or you don't!'

'Of course I trust you! It's just . . . ' She broke off miserably. How could she tell him every smile and word he shared with Rosamund fired her jealousy, because that smile or word was not for *her*?

'When we were young, folk had Rosie and me pegged as sweethearts. I can guess at the gossip when both of us left Blackthorn suddenly as we did. And I don't doubt tongues were clacking again when she came home for Christmas. You have to understand, Meirian, Rosie was my best friend years ago. Yet I turned my back on her. I walked away when she needed me most.' He confessed bleakly, 'I wouldn't blame her if she hated the sight of me now, but she doesn't. Rosie hasn't a bitter bone in her body. She has a generous and forgiving heart.'

'She does seem a very gentle person,' admitted Meirian, adding truthfully, 'I liked her.'

'I could see the pair of you were getting along well.' He smiled. 'And Daisy took a real shine to you.'

'She's a lovely child,' Meirian said, returning his smile. 'I think my saddle and harness might've won her over.'

James rose, standing before the desk and gazing down at Meirian, brushing a stray wisp of chestnut hair from her forehead. 'Will you come to the play at Kirkgate? I promise to buy you a posy and a box of Turkish delight.'

'I'd like to come very much . . . ' she said, her pulse quickening as James raised her hand to his lips and slowly kissed her fingertips and palm. 'But — but only because of the Turkish delight, mind!'

* * *

It had been a quite wonderful evening. Although the box of Turkish delight

remained unopened, Meirian's fingertips oft strayed to the fragrant posy of
winter flowers during the long drive
from the theatre through the dark
starless night.

'You hurry away indoors,' James said
when they returned to the manor
house. 'I told Alf not to wait up for us,
so I need to feed Bessie and put her in
for the night.'

'I'll help you.' Accepting his hand
down from the wagon, she started into
the stable and froze in her tracks.
'James!'

'I see him!' James moved swiftly
ahead of her, resting a reassuring hand
to the quivering shoulder of Lyall's bay.
'Easy, Tam! Easy, now . . .'

His hand came away wet, and when
Meirian lit the lantern, they saw the
animal was wide-eyed and sweating,
still saddled and trailing his reins. He
was streaked with mud and dirt, his
head, chest and sides flecked with foam
and blood.

'Poor beggar's been ridden hard and

just left,' muttered James, already stripping off the saddle and bridle. 'What the hell's Lyall thinking about, leaving his horse in this state? While I rub him down, will you see to Bessie?'

Meirian nodded, bringing the placid mare into the stable and settling her into her stall. 'I wonder why Lyall's ridden back? He's not supposed to be coming home until after his exhibition next week.'

James shook his head in disgust, working quickly and quietly with the exhausted bay. 'I've no idea what's going on, but it can't be good.'

'Bessie's all done,' said Meirian presently, patting the mare's broad neck as she ate. 'I'll go and see what Lyall's up to, shall I?'

'Good idea.' He was on his knees, examining a bloody wound on the bay's flank. 'I'll be a while yet. Tam's got a deep gorse cut that needs tending.'

Meirian found Lyall in the drawing-room, seated before the dying fire with his elbows propped on his knees, his head slumped into his hands.

'Who's there?' He started violently, blinking in the sudden brightness from her candle. 'Oh, it's you, Meirian.'

'Whatever's wrong?' she asked, swallowing her alarm at his wide distracted eyes and the tears coursing unhindered from them. 'Are you ill?'

'I've been such a fool!' he blurted brokenly. 'Stupid, stupid, stupid! Why didn't I — ah, I feel so angry! So furious! I could have prevented this, and I did nothing. *Nothing!*'

She dropped to her knees, so their faces were on a level. 'Tell me what's happened, Lyall.'

'Ambrose Mather has withdrawn his patronage.' He dragged out in a shuddering breath. 'He threw me out of his house. Said he wouldn't rest until he saw me ruined.'

Meirian's mind was reeling. What on earth had gone on at the industrialist's mansion in Preston? She was aware the Mathers had marriageable daughters. Had there perhaps been some sort of unfortunate liason, or worse . . . ?

'I've brought it upon myself, that's what makes it unbearable. I behaved shamefully.' His eyes were empty now, devoid of emotion. 'And I'm paying for it by losing everything I've ever wanted.'

'Your exhibition!' gasped Meirian, suddenly registering the implications of Ambrose Mather's action. 'What will you do now?'

'What *can* I do?' he snapped bitterly. 'Without Mather, there won't *be* an exhibition! He was paying for it all. Arranging it all. Several influential people from the art world have already attended a private showing and made offers to buy four of my paintings. Critics from the journals and newspapers were there, too. They were very favourably impressed. I've actually seen the reviews they intend publishing! Full of praise and recognition for a new talent . . . I had it all, Meirian.' His voice was broken, barely audible, as though all energy and passion were

314

spent. 'I was mere days away from having everything I've ever dreamed about in the palm of my hand!'

'You can't stay down here, it's freezing,' she murmured at length, eyeing the cold grey coals. 'Go on up to bed and I'll bring you some tea. Are you hungry? I'll be fixing something for James and myself, so it's no trouble.'

'James?' he echoed, glancing at her sidelong and noticing her hat and coat. 'Have you been out?'

'Mmm. To see a play. We found Tam in the stables, that's how we knew you must be home.'

'Tam . . . I'd forgotten all about him.'

'James is taking care of him.' She straightened up, drawing Lyall to standing also. 'You're exhausted. You need to rest. Things won't seem quite so black in the morning.'

'If only that were true!' His dark eyes were filled with despair. He gazed down at her for a long moment, before clasping her hands within his own. 'Thank you, Meirian. You're wonderful.

I've never known anybody like you.'

Smiling gently, she slipped her hands free. 'I'll make that tea.'

Returning the smile, he shambled from the room, pausing at the foot of the stairs to look back at her. 'Please don't mention this to James or to Ma. I'll tell them myself. That's going to be the hardest part. You see, they've always believed in me and had utter faith in my talent . . . and now I've let them down!'

A short while later, when Meirian tapped on his door and took in a tray of tea and freshly made toast, Lyall had washed and changed. It was quite a transformation, for his appearance and mood were much improved. Crossing the room to set down the tray, Meirian's skirts brushed the edge of the bed covers, and a small glass bottle rolled from the quilt onto the floor. Bending to retrieve it, she placed the bottle onto the dresser beside the tray.

'Sleeping draught. Henry gave some to me a while ago,' Lyall said, slipping the bottle into his pocket. 'I thought I needed a good sleep tonight.'

'You'll feel all the better for it, too,' she replied, pouring the tea. 'Have this while it's hot.'

'Thank you again for all you've done,' he said, sitting on the edge of the bed. 'You know, since we were talking earlier, I've been thinking. The exhibition is less than a week away. Everything's been done. Invitations, publicity, catalogues, everything. Why *shouldn't* it go ahead as planned?'

'I don't understand. You said Mr Mather has withdrawn his patronage.'

'He has. However, a great many things have already been paid for, so Mather can't do anything about those. All I need to do is find sufficient funds to pay the remainder of the bills, and my exhibition will go ahead as arranged.'

'Can you do that?'

'Why not?' he demanded, on his feet now, pacing the floor as possibilities came rushing to him.

'I'm certain James will — ' Meirian began.

Lyall shook his head vehemently. 'I wouldn't borrow from James. Nor Ma, either. Not even if they could afford it, which they can't. The family has land, but we've never had much money. And just now, James is working hard to repay all Father's debts. No, I must do this on my own,' he went on excitedly. 'Actually, I probably won't need to borrow money at all. If one rich, successful industrialist was willing to invest in my work and talent, why not others?'

'Lyall, you must take care — '

'Don't worry about me!' he reassured cheerfully, brushing her cheek with a kiss. 'I'm going to put on my own exhibition. And you, dear Meirian, shall be the guest of honour!'

* * *

What with running the school, doing her own work at the manor house and keeping up with her regular duties about the village, Meirian didn't have a spare moment. She'd hardly seen Lyall. He still hadn't told the family about his trouble with Ambrose Mather, and that made Meirian feel distinctly uncomfortable, not least when Isabelle sought her out at the schoolhouse after the children had gone home for the day.

'Lyall confides in you,' Isabelle said, sitting at one of the benches while Meirian tidied up the classroom. 'A couple of days ago, he went to Kirkgate cock-a-hoop and full of confidence, only to return morose and disturbed. Today, he's driven to Liverpool with Tod Weir — '

'Lyall has gone with Tod Weir?' echoed Meirian sharply. 'Why would he do that?'

Isabelle shrugged. 'It's one of Weir's regular trips on estate business. When I asked Lyall the purpose of *his* visit, he mumbled something incoherent and marched off. I take it you don't know the reason either?'

'I only wish I did, ma'am.' Meirian

frowned. She'd witnessed too many acrimonious exchanges between the two men not to be deeply anxious. 'I knew nothing of it.'

'Lyall's exhibition opens in a matter of days. Whyever has he come back from Preston now? James doesn't know anything,' went on Isabelle in exasperation. 'Have *you* any idea what's going on — or does my asking place you in an awkward position? Ah, I see it does.' She smiled ruefully, rising from the bench. 'My apologies, Meirian. I'll enquire no further.'

★　★　★

Returning from Liverpool with the coach — for Tod Weir was remaining in the town a while longer — Lyall sojourned at the manor house only to bathe, change his clothes and have supper before leaving for Preston. During the meal, he briefly mentioned parting company with Ambrose Mather and declared his exhibition would proceed as planned. He'd expect the family to arrive in Preston on the day of the opening. Rooms were booked for them all at The White Hart so they might rest and change and dine. Everything was arranged perfectly.

After supper, Meirian followed him out to the stables. 'Your explanation to the family was sketchy, to say the least,' she began at once. 'Have you found another patron?'

Lyall looked at her, then turned away and shook his head. 'I trailed around Kirkgate and called upon everybody I could think of. Nobody was interested. I had to borrow the money.'

'However will you pay it back?' she exclaimed, horrified. Having been brought up with a fear of debt and its consequences, the very notion of being indebted filled Meirian with dread.

*   *   *

'You told me yourself you have no money! It's not just the sum you've borrowed, either. There'll be interest to pay as well!'

'You recall my mentioning that several people wished to buy my pictures?' he replied mildly. 'After the paintings are sold, I'll be able to repay the loan.'

'They put debtors in gaol,' she muttered, adding almost as an after-thought, 'Where exactly does Tod Weir fit in to this scheme of yours? Why did you go to Liverpool with him?'

'I needed money urgently, Meirian, and time was short,' he answered ruefully. 'Weir's bankers are in Liver-pool.'

'Oh, no!' she breathed in dismay. 'To become indebted to such a man as Tod Weir!'

'My whole life, my whole future, were at stake! I was desperate,' he murmured gravely, meeting her eyes. 'Beggars can't be choosers. I either borrowed the money or lost my exhibition. I had no choice — Tod Weir was my only resort!'

★ ★ ★

The exhibition could not properly be deemed a failure, since nobody save Lyall Caunce's family came to view his paintings. Those distinguished guests who had so readily accepted invitations from Ambrose Mather did not attend. The critical reviews that had originally showered praise and promise upon the unknown young artist were rewritten, appearing in print to ridicule and dismiss his work in the most humiliating fashion. The reach and influence of a rich, powerful man like Ambrose Mather was ubiquitous and ruthless. Lyall's reputation was indeed ruined, his career as a painter over before it began.

The whole family had a sombre journey home, however only Lyall and Meirian realised the full import of the disaster that had occurred. Upon arrival at the manor house, Lyall immediately left the others and strode into the woods towards the mere.

'Wait!' she cried, hurrying after him and catching his fingers. 'Don't go off on your own! Come up to the house!'

'I can't look anybody in the eye, Meirian. I can't stand their pitying me!' He got out miserably. 'They mean well, but — I'm going over to the island.'

'Will you be all right?'

'I need to . . . I don't know what I'm to do, Meirian!' He pushed a hand through his dark hair, his gaze slipping beyond her to the cold grey waters of the mere. 'I've always been certain about my painting. About my purpose in life. Now that's gone. It's all over.'

'No, it isn't!' she protested fiercely. 'You'll continue painting! With time, you'll get over this setback. Meanwhile, you must find a way of repaying Tod Weir's loan. You have to break free of him, Lyall! You must, or he'll destroy you.'

'As he destroyed my father,' returned Lyall bitterly, turning from her and walking slowly between the trees to the banks of Swallowhole Mere.

* ★ ★

After church on Sunday, James fell into step beside Meirian as they followed Henry and Isabelle across the bleak frosty churchyard.

'Lyall's coping better than I expected,' he remarked quietly. 'What do you make of his plan to go to Italy and make a fresh start?'

'It's what artists do, I suppose. Go abroad to study and paint. First of all, though, he has to — ' She broke off, amending her words. Only she and Lyall knew of his debt to Tod Weir. 'Well, Italy's for the future, isn't it?'

'From the way he's talking,' replied James, 'Lyall regards it the very *near* future.'

'I haven't seen Tod Weir for a few days,' she commented thoughtfully. 'Is he still in Liverpool?'

'I expected him back before now, but he's not shown up yet,' answered James with annoyance. 'He comes and goes from Blackthorn however he pleases, and never a mind that he has a job to do here! If he's not back by tomorrow, I'll have to go to Kirkgate myself.' He went on, pausing as an idea struck him. 'Meirian, you've finished at the school, haven't you?'

She nodded. 'Mr Legh took over last week.'

'Perfect! Why don't we go to Kirkgate together? Make a day of it?' He grinned down at her. 'My business at the grain merchant's will take barely an hour. We can have luncheon at The Running Horses and I'll show you around the town. It's a pretty little place, and you've never seen the castle in daylight.'

'Will we be skating there?' she asked, her eyes dancing.

''Think we'd best travel by wagon this time,' he replied, taking her hand as they crunched through frosty fallen leaves on the beech avenue. 'Although we'll likely find an orchard to bide a while.'

★　★　★

Meirian awoke even earlier than usual the next morning, snuggling blissfully within the soft warmth of her comfortable bed. A whole day with James stretched before her!

Clad in her best coat and bonnet, she was in the study finishing off one or two things when Joe brought in the morning's post. Glancing through the letters as usual, she paused at one addressed to James, instantly recognising Rosamund Petherbridge's handwriting. She remembered that neat, sloping feminine script from the thank-you letter Rosamund had sent after her family's Christmastide visit at Blackthorn.

'All set for the off?' James put his head around the door, his deep blue eyes smiling at Meirian in a way that tore into her senses. 'It's bitterly cold, so . . .'

Without a word, she proffered the letter. He took it from her, glancing curiously at the handwriting before breaking the seal. Meirian watched the laughter in his eyes fade; saw a frown appear and deepen on his forehead. Gripped by an irrational foreboding, she could only stand impotently while James scanned the neat lines, and wait in an agony of apprehension as mere seconds stretched endlessly.

'Rosie's coming back.' He snapped his gaze from the letter, crushing it into his pocket and looking to Meirian. 'We'll have to go to Kirkgate another day.'

'What — what about your business there?' was all she could say.

'It'll have to wait. This is more important.' He was already gone from the study and starting along the passage, his last words coming to her on a blast of icy air as he flung open the massive oak door. 'I'm driving up to The Three Crowns to meet Rosie's coach!'

Still dressed for her journey, Meirian sank down behind her desk. She wasn't sure how long she remained there, staring at her cold hands tightly clasped upon the blotter, the small pile of mail beside it completely forgotten.

'Oh, miss! Thank heavens I've found you — I thought you'd be gone by now!' exclaimed Gladys, bursting in through the open doorway. 'It's Becky Beswick — he's at the garden door, asking for you. I think you'd best come quick!'

When Meirian reached the garden, she saw Becky resting against the huge stone horse trough. He rose at once, crossing the yard to her side.

'It's Tod Weir,' he began simply. 'Me and the lad have just found him in the ice-house. He's dead, missy. Has been a fair while, if I'm any judge.'

12

'I know it's wrong to speak ill of the dead, Meirian,' Rosamund Petherbridge murmured as the two women walked slowly through the ice-shrouded garden after Tod Weir's funeral. Daisy was skipping on ahead of them, pulling along her rag-doll and Pierrot on the little sledge James had made for the child's toys. 'I'm glad he's gone. He was a loathsome man and he frightened me.'

'I'd never really thought about your knowing Weir,' remarked Meirian, smiling fondly at the happy sight of Daisy standing on her tiptoes and showing her doll the glittering icicles dripping from the bare oak. 'But of course, you must've known him when you were all growing up.'

'We always kept out of his way when we were children. Although it wasn't until considerably later I found out what Tod Weir was really capable of,' recalled Rosamund, distractedly voicing her thoughts. 'Last week, when I wrote to James and told him I was coming back to Blackthorn, I was certain Tod Weir was responsible for ... for something that has recently occurred. Now I have no idea. None whatsoever.'

Rosamund's words wouldn't have made any sense to Meirian, even had she been paying full attention. As it was, she was lost in the turmoil and confusion of her own thoughts. Rosamund clearly had not the slightest inkling of Meirian's feelings for James, nor of his for her — if indeed James had spoken sincerely when he'd declared his affection. And it wasn't that Meirian distrusted him exactly, it was just . . .

From under lowered lids, Meirian glanced sidelong at her companion. Within moments of receiving Rosamund's letter, James had abandoned their plans for spending the day together in Kirkgate, and the business he had there, to rush off to The Three Crowns and bring home his childhood sweetheart!

Rosamund and Daisy had been travelling alone. Jonathan was not with them, nor was he to follow. Ostensibly, he was prosecuting a long and complex case at the high court and so couldn't accompany his family. There had been no mention of how long mother and daughter — *James's* daughter — were to remain under the manor house roof. Although Meirian had never witnessed any outward show of romantic affection between the couple, the deep attachment they shared was clear for all to see. And there had been several occasions when she'd glimpsed them alone and ensconced in intimate conversation.

' . . . wouldn't wish it on your worst enemy. Such a horrible way to die, wasn't it?'

'Hmm?' Meirian started from her reverie. 'Yes, indeed it was. Dr Poulsom — your father, I mean — said Weir must've fallen down the shaft and cracked his head on the ice. It was quite a long drop, I believe.'

Rosamund shuddered, as much from the image in her mind as the freezing weather. 'Have you ever been inside the ice-house? Oh, it's a horrible, claustro-phobic place! Like a great brick bottomless pit buried under the earth so you'd never even guess it existed. During wintertime, the pit is stacked with blocks of ice and the walls are absolutely sheer. It's a dangerous place, so the men always work there in pairs.'

'Tod Weir was evidently alone. Your father couldn't say when the accident might have happened, because of the intense cold in there,' remarked Meir-ian as they gave the ice-house a wide berth and wound through the stand of alders back towards the warm, welcom-ing lights and smoking chimneys of the manor house. 'Blackthorn will get a new bailiff, and whoever James chooses has to be a tremendous improvement.'

'There wasn't anybody of his own at

the funeral, was there? Family, or true friends. Yet Weir was born here on the estate, you know,' mused Rosamund, catching hold of Daisy's mittened hand as they walked. 'In the old gamekeeper's cottage where Annie Wilcox and her children are living.'

'Really?'

'Oh, yes. Tod Weir knew Blackthorn and its doings inside out. Lived here his whole life. Yet has anyone genuinely mourned his passing?'

'I doubt it,' replied Meirian bluntly. 'He reaped what he sowed. James and I will be going to his cottage in a day or two to empty it and pack up Weir's possessions.'

'Did he have relatives anywhere?'

Meirian shook her head. 'Not really. Mrs Caunce recalled mention of a distant cousin somewhere away over on the east coast. Whoever he is, he's in for a nice windfall. By all accounts, Tod Weir was a wealthy man!'

★ ★ ★

It seemed an age, part of another lifetime, since Meirian had first set eyes upon Tod Weir's cottage that dark, stormy night she'd arrived in Blackthorn with James. Now the bailiff's cottage buried deep in the woods stood empty, washed with cold, brilliant winter light. Everywhere was still and eerily silent, for Alf had already taken the horses up to the stables at the manor house.

'Are you sure you've no objections to doing this?' enquired James, glancing down at her as they made to enter. 'Very well. Let's get it over with. We'll pack everything into the boxes ready to be sent on to Weir's cousin. Oh, and keep a look-out for any papers or letters with the cousin's address on. Failing that, it'll be for the lawyers to trace him.'

They worked methodically and mostly without conversation, packing and loading the boxes onto the wagon, stacking the furniture, gradually stripping the cottage of its contents. They unearthed a small locked cupboard concealed behind the bedstead.

'No money in here. He must've kept it all in the bank,' commented James after breaking open the sturdy cupboard door. 'Only papers. Letters from Weir's bankers in Liverpool, a deed for some land down at Crosby, more letters ... See if there's anything from the cousin while I nail up this last box.'

Meirian came upon a document bearing Lyall's signature and the terms of the loan. She nearly gasped out loud at the sum involved, and at the amount of interest the ruthless bailiff had set. Lyall would've had to sell a great many paintings at extraordinarily high prices to have any hope of ever clearing such a debt! Impulsively, she crushed the agreement into her pocket and continued sifting through the bundle of papers. Amongst the bills of sale, invoices and so on, there was no personal correspondence whatsoever, and nothing bearing the name of Weir's only relative.

Reaching into the cupboard for the oilskin wallet propped up at the back, her fingers touched upon a small wooden chest concealed behind it. Withdrawing it, she raised the lid. The chest contained six rows of small glass bottles, corked and unlabelled, and identical to the one Lyall had had in his room upon that night he'd ridden hard from Preston. He'd told Meirian the bottle contained a sleeping draught prescribed by Henry Poulsom, but he'd lied. She could see there had originally been thirty-six bottles in this chest; a dozen were now missing. With a sinking heart, Meirian guessed who had taken possession of those bottles.

James heard her involuntary sigh of despair and crossed the cottage to her side, taking the heavy little chest from her hands.

'So *this* was one of Weir's dealings! My God, why didn't I realise?'

'What is it, exactly?'

'I'd say it's a very particular sort of laudanum,' he replied bitterly, taking the chest to the hearth and tumbling the bottles so they smashed, spilling their infernal contents over the cold coals and spent kindling. 'Highly prized and handsomely paid for by those who seek the pleasure or comfort it gives them.'

'I have heard of such intoxicants,' murmured Meirian, staring at the spreading liquid with revulsion. 'It's wicked to make money from other people's neediness.'

'It's a bad business, all right. And it explains a lot.' James turned from the hearth, striding to the open doorway and standing on the stoop, as though needing to breathe in fresh unadulterated air. 'Before I left Blackthorn, I was too young and didn't have the experience to recognise the signs, but finding that stuff now and looking back . . . It's quite obvious! Tod Weir was always very good at supplying my father with a great deal of whatever he fancied, Meirian. I'd always known about the women and the contraband brandy, but

I never even suspected this!' He cast a distraught glance to the remains of the smashed bottles before meeting her eyes, his face grave. 'Pa depended more and more upon Weir until, piece by piece, he'd taken control of Blackthorn. And my father . . . Well, he was too preoccupied to notice, much less care, that his bailiff was bleeding the manor dry. It must've been a real shock to Weir when Pa killed himself and I came home to take over the estate.'

Meirian saw the glint of unshed tears in James's eyes, and went to his side. She'd been on the brink of confiding her suspicions about Lyall and the laudanum, however this wasn't the time. 'There isn't much more to do. Shall we finish up here?'

'The sooner the better,' he responded gruffly, striding indoors once more. 'Small wonder Weir spent so much time in Liverpool! He'd be collecting that stuff from ships coming in from the East. It was probably one of his more lucrative dealings.'

'At least it's over now, James,' she murmured, touching her hand to his as they closed the cottage door behind them, and praying her suspicions about Lyall were unfounded.

* * *

When Lyall had taken her across to Hermitage upon one of her early visits to the island, he had insisted upon teaching Meirian to sail the sculler. She hadn't shown much enthusiasm at the time, because she'd never envisaged herself sailing alone across Swallowhole Mere! Now, however, as she pushed the little craft onto the smooth water, she welcomed the independence the skill gave her. On this occasion, she wouldn't have wanted James or even Alf to accompany her. She needed to see Lyall privately.

'How was the crossing?' he said, meeting her on the steps of the lodge. 'It looked very smooth from here.'

'Yes, it was,' she said soberly, taking

the loan contract from her pocket and offering it to him. 'James and I were clearing out Tod Weir's cottage. I found this amongst his papers.'

Lyall glanced at it cursorily. 'Has James seen this? Good. There's no need for anybody to know about the debt now. Just as well, really. Folk might start wondering if Tod Weir's death was an unfortunate accident after all!'

She watched him go to the fireplace and allow the document to fall amongst the hungry flames. 'You'd never have been able to pay back that money, would you?'

'I suppose not,' he admitted, watching the paper burn. 'I was so desperate to show my paintings, I'd have sold my soul to the devil.'

'Isn't that exactly what you did?' she asked coldly. 'Except Weir died before the day of reckoning?'

Lyall stared at her, unable to read her expression. 'Meirian, you surely can't believe I . . . Yes, I'm glad he's dead, and it's true Weir and I met sometimes at the ice-house — '

'Is that where the pair of you traded laudanum or whatever it is?' she demanded. 'We found quite a store of little glass bottles. Just like your sleeping draught!'

'I'm truly sorry for deceiving you, Meirian. I did want to tell you the truth, but I was ashamed,' he murmured simply, avoiding her eyes. 'By then, I couldn't — *can't* — get by without the damnable stuff. I despise myself for my weakness, but I felt like I was drowning in an awful, consuming darkness. Day after day was filled with remorse and utter despair. I had no hope, no faith. There was nothing left. In the end, I just couldn't bear the pain any longer.'

Meirian sat across the hearth from him, searching his earnest face and the tormented depths of the troubled, restless dark eyes. 'How did it start?' she said gently. 'Was it — was it during those bad dreams about your father's death?'

'You saw what I was like then,' he confided miserably. 'I feared I was losing my mind. I couldn't rest, couldn't paint, and every night those wretched dreams about Pa . . . Weir saw me standing by Swallowhole one day. Said he had a tonic that'd make me feel better.'

'You didn't know what he was selling you?' she exclaimed.

'I may not have known precisely.' He grinned ruefully. 'But I knew well enough it wasn't the kind of tonic I'd get from Henry. Once I'd started looking forward to Weir bringing the little bottles from Liverpool for me, well, he had my soul then, didn't he? I realised too late that history was repeating itself. Weir was set to destroy me exactly as he destroyed Pa. He did, you know.' Lyall raised fierce eyes, burning with anger and regret. 'He killed my father as surely as if he'd put the noose around Pa's neck himself!'

They sat without speaking as time ticked away. At length, Meirian broke the silence. 'James told me he'd asked you to be bailiff, so the two of you might run the estate together. It's a fine idea. Will you accept?'

'I'm going to Italy,' he answered quietly. 'To paint. To start afresh. To make a good, fulfilling life far from the malicious influence of Ambrose Mather and his lackeys.'

'Won't all that be terribly expensive?' she ventured practically. 'Wouldn't it be better to work here with James — '

'I no longer have any debts, and I've already made my plans,' he interrupted softly.

'What about your studio here on the island?' she protested. 'And all your paintings — what's to become of them?'

'They haven't been unpacked since coming back from Preston. I'll send for them when I'm settled.' He smiled across at her. 'My mind is quite made up, Meirian. Come spring, I'll be in Italy.'

★ ★ ★

With a heavy heart, Meirian returned to the manor house as the shadows of the winter afternoon lengthened into a moonless evening. Taking the shortcut through the walled garden, she froze there in the twilight. The drawing-room was brightly illuminated, and through the long window she saw James and Rosamund standing within. They were talking earnestly, she gazing up into his face, he touching a tender hand to her shoulder, quite unaware they were being observed from the dusky garden.

When James took Rosamund into his arms, holding her tightly against him, his cheek against the softness of her auburn hair, Meirian could bear it no longer. Racing from the garden, into the house and along the passageway, she burst into the drawing-room — and was taken aback to find James alone now, his boot leaning on the hearth as he gazed broodingly into the fire.

'What cruel game are you playing, James?' she exploded, facing him with eyes blazing. 'I *saw* you — making love to Rosamund!'

He stared at her incredulously. 'I was comforting her, Meirian! She's upset. Rosie has troubles, if you must know.'

'*Troubles*, you say?' she echoed sceptically. 'Is that why she's here without her husband?'

'That's none of your business.' James's piercing blue eyes sparked dangerously. 'It's Rosie's affair, nobody else's.'

'Isn't it *your* affair too, James?'

'What's got into you today?' He shook his head in disbelief. 'You're not making any sense!'

'Aren't I? Then let me say it plainly,' she cried. 'Rosamund Poulsom was your childhood sweetheart — everybody tells me so — and now she's here alone with her daughter! Is Daisy *your* daughter too, James — *Is she?*'

Meirian blanched at the sudden charged tension within the comfortable drawing-room. James was glaring at her as though she'd struck him, but she stood her ground, utterly determined now that truth be out. Nonetheless, her voice was a little unsteady as she added, 'That's what folk are saying — and Daisy *does* look like you!'

'Folk'll say any old nonsense,' he snapped. 'If you mean Daisy has fair hair and blue eyes, so do many children — I'm not *their* father, either!'

Striding past without sparing Meirian another glance, James quit the room and noiselessly closed the door, leaving her alone and spent. Suddenly weak at the knees, she sank down into the chair beside the window, resting her head against the wing and gazing unseeing into the dark garden, hot tears spilling unbidden and unnoticed from her eyes.

She scarcely heard a gentle tapping at the door, nor was aware of Rosamund's entering until she put a gentle hand upon Meirian's trembling shoulder.

'Forgive me, but I overheard you and James quarrelling,' she began softly. 'I owe you an apology — and an explanation. Could we perhaps go to your room, where we might speak privately?'

Upstairs, Meirian bathed her eyes and tidied her hair, striving to compose herself for whatever she was about to hear, while Rosamund was busy fetching tea. When she came in with the tray, Meirian was seated at the fireside and prepared to learn the truth and whatever her future might hold.

'I am so very sorry for the distress my returning to Blackthorn has caused you, Meirian,' she began at once, pouring the tea. 'I had no idea you were in love with James, or I would have spoken sooner. I can well imagine how all this must appear, but appearances can deceive. While James and I had been the closest of friends, we were never lovers.'

Meirian's heart was pounding. 'Then — then Daisy isn't James's child!'

Rosamund shook her head. 'I love my husband dearly, Meirian, and always shall. Until last Christmastide, only

Jonathan knew the truth about Daisy. Then when I saw James again, I told him too. We'd parted acrimoniously all those years ago. I needed to set things right between us. I owed James that, and now I owe it to you, too.'

'You don't owe me at all, Rosamund,' she put in softly. 'I just don't understand why James couldn't have said something himself.'

'He's a loyal, honourable man who could never betray a friend or their secrets,' she said, drawing in a steadying breath. 'When I was fifteen, I had an affair with Donald Caunce.'

Meirian's jaw dropped. 'With — with James's *father*!'

'We met in secret at the lodge on Hermitage Island. I was vain and foolish and selfish. I fancied I loved him and believed he loved me. I wrote him long and indiscreet letters,' went on Rosamund, her eyes fixed upon the tea tray. 'Donald must've taken the amethyst necklace from Aunt Isabelle's jewel casket, because he presented it to me. I'd wear it for him when we were alone together.'

'Did Mrs Caunce, and your father — did they find out?'

'To this day, they don't know about it, and I pray they never will. Nobody suspected a thing.' She swallowed hard, remembering. 'Then, quite by chance, one afternoon James walked into the lodge and discovered me with his father . . . '

'Oh!' was all Meirian could say.

'James was furious. He fought with his father and left Blackthorn without a word.'

So many things James had told Meirian now took on deeper meaning for her. She sighed, reaching out to touch Rosamund's cold hand.

'When I believed I might be with child, I told Donald and he said he'd get Tod Weir to arrange everything,' went on Rosamund soberly. 'That was the last time I ever saw Donald. I went away to stay with my aunt in Carlisle, and met Jonathan. He's a good, decent man, Meirian! We're so very happy together.' She choked back a sudden overwhelming sob. 'And now, somehow, I have to find a way to save our marriage and preserve Jonathan's career and reputation!'

★ ★ ★

Meirian excused herself from Rosamund's company as quickly as she was able and sought out James. He was in the stables, sitting alone at the bench and repairing a worn piece of Bessie's harness in the flickering glow of the lantern.

'Becky taught me to do this, y'know,' he commented matter-of-factly when she burst into the quiet stable. 'A man of many skills, is Becky Beswick.'

'I'm sure,' said Meirian, dragging a bale of hay and sitting before him. 'Why didn't you tell me Rosamund was being blackmailed?'

That got his full attention!

'Rosamund's told me everything. I'm

very sorry I thought what I did about you, James,' she rushed on earnestly. 'It's not that I didn't trust you, it's just . . . Well, I suppose it's because I love you and was scared of losing you.'

'That's all right, then,' he remarked, setting the harness aside before slowly drawing Meirian up from the hay bale onto his lap and into his arms. 'Because I couldn't imagine my life without you in it . . . '

Some while later, they started from the stables, the blackmailer's threats once more uppermost in their conversation.

'It's common knowledge Jonathan Petherbridge is to be made a judge, but any breath of scandal would put paid to his appointment to the bench. If it gets out his wife's had an affair and borne another man's child, Jonathan could be forced to resign from his chambers and cease being a practising barrister altogether,' James said gravely. 'More important still is the necessity of protecting Daisy from being hurt. Ma and Henry, too. They don't know Jonathan isn't her real father.'

'And now, all these years later, Rosamund has received a message demanding money in exchange for the return of her love letters to Donald Caunce.' Meirian shook her head in disbelief. 'Whatever does her husband say about it all?'

'She hasn't told him yet. Jonathan's not been too well of late, and he's already under a lot of strain leading the prosecution in a capital trial at Lancaster,' explained James. 'Rosie didn't want to worry him, so she sold some of her jewellery and paid up. Needless to say, she didn't get her letters back, but she *did* receive another message demanding even more money! It was then Rosie wrote to me and came home to Blackthorn. There was nobody else she could turn to.'

'Have you any idea who's blackmailing her?'

James shook his head grimly. 'We need to find out, though, and get those love letters back — before an entire family is torn apart!'

* * *

Meirian, James and Rosamund sat up until the small hours. When exhausted and no nearer finding an answer or solution, despite all their deliberations, they finally retired to their beds. Meirian slept almost at once, stirring after only a few hours and immediately wide awake. It was still dark of course, and bone-numbingly cold. A hard, dark coldness without the whiteness of frost or ice to lighten and brighten the early morning. Her fire was almost out, and, wrapping the quilt tight about her, she reluctantly clambered from the high bed to add more coal and kindling. After coaxing it into a comforting little blaze, she sat before the grate warming her feet and hands and mulling over all they'd said. Then suddenly it came to her, as vivid as a tableau set before her eyes!

Tossing the quilt aside, she dressed hurriedly and sped from her room and downstairs, passing Hafwen as she went.

''Morning, lovey! Miss Rosamund's in the kitchen and — '

'Sorry, Haffie!' called Meirian, not breaking her stride. 'Tell Rosamund I'll see her later — there's something I have to do straightaway!'

Hafwen stared after her cousin as she sprinted past the Great Hall and out through the old oak door. 'Wherever are you going in such a rush?'

'Hermitage Island!'

$$\star \quad \star \quad \star$$

Dawn was breaking, and Swallowhole Mere was as clear and smooth as a looking-glass. Not a breath of breeze ruffled the deep silvery water or stirred the feathery reeds as Meirian took the sculler slowly and surely across to Hermitage Island. Lyall was waiting for her on the sloping bank, hauling the little boat up from the shallows and helping her ashore.

'Good morning! What a wonderful surprise!' he greeted her with a wide smile. 'I saw you coming from my window and set an extra cup and breakfast dish.'

Meirian walked beside him up into the lodge before speaking out. 'Are you blackmailing Rosamund?'

She waited — *hoped* — for an indignant denial. None came. Lyall moved from her, past the table set for breakfast, to sit in the alcove beneath his father's duelling pistols and next to the walnut bureau where he'd so recently come upon the amethyst necklace — and that treacherous bundle of love letters.

'It's a rotten thing to do. I had no choice, you see.' He spread his hands in a helpless gesture. 'After the exhibition, I'd lost everything. I had that huge, impossible debt to Tod Weir. I was desperate. Trapped. There was no way out . . . Then I remembered the letters.'

'And used them to threaten an old friend!' said Meirian contemptuously. 'Have you any idea of the anguish you're causing Rosamund?'

'I'll never send her letters to the newspapers or to the judiciary. I wouldn't hurt Rosamund or her family,' he responded dismissively. 'It's an empty threat and it hasn't done any real harm. Jonathan Petherbridge is a wealthy man. They won't even miss the money.'

'Done no harm — ? Can't you see — ' She broke off as another horrifying possibility seared across her mind. 'Tod Weir ... You and he sometimes met at the ice-house, didn't you?'

'His death was an accident.' Lyall shrugged. 'Although if anybody else but you and I knew about my debt and read that contract you found in Weir's cottage, they'd doubtless believe I had a first-class motive for murder, wouldn't they?'

Meirian stared at him, her throat dry.

'Give me Rosamund's letters, Lyall. All of them. You must stop these cruel threats immediately.'

'I can't. Not yet. I need more money for my removal to Italy.'

'For heaven's sake, you've got away with the debt to Tod Weir!' she exclaimed impatiently. 'Why don't you take James's offer of bailiff? As well as helping your brother, you'd actually earn enough to travel to Italy in the future.'

'I'm leaving for Italy within the next few weeks, Meirian,' he replied calmly. 'I want you to come with me.'

'What?'

He rose, taking the couple of steps that separated them and catching hold of her shoulders. 'You must know I love you, Meirian! I believe I've loved you since that first moment we met in Hafwen's kitchen. Marry me!' he murmured softly, his dark eyes deep and unfathomable. 'Be my wife and come to Italy with me. We'll have the most wonderful life — '

'Marry you?' She drew free of his touch, shaking her head and turning away from him. 'I could never marry you, Lyall!'

'It's James, isn't it? Isn't it?' he demanded angrily, gripping her fore-arms so fiercely his fingers dug painfully into her flesh. 'It's *always* James! I wanted Rosamund, but she was too busy chasing James to ever notice me! And now *you* — '

'Please let me go.' Meirian fought to keep fear and panic from her voice. 'Why don't we go back to the manor house together and — '

'Set her free, Lyall!'

James's calm, clear voice was but yards away. Meirian hadn't noticed the lodge door opening, and relief coursed through her when she glanced around and saw him standing there.

'We can sort everything out between ourselves,' he went on easily, taking even, measured strides towards his younger brother. 'Nobody but us need ever — '

'No!' Meirian glimpsed Lyall's quick, darting movement to the alcove and his father's duelling pistols. '*No!*'

Shoving her roughly down across the couch, Lyall levelled one pistol at her while reaching up for the second, his dark eyes never leaving his elder brother's face.

'I'm sorry it's ending this way, James. I truly don't want to hurt anyone,' he murmured, keeping Meirian in his sights as he slowly edged around towards the door. 'But if you try to stop me, I *will* shoot. I have no choice and nothing left to lose!'

The door slammed, the key turned, and Lyall was gone.

'For pity's sake, James,' cried Meirian as he immediately went to the door, 'let him go! He might have killed us both, the mood he's in!'

'That's exactly why I have to stop him!' Taking hold of a chair, James smashed the window glass, knocking it clear from its frame. 'Stay here, Meirian.'

'James!'

It took her a few precious seconds to scramble out over the ledge and take off down the slope after him. She caught up as James stood hopelessly at the water's edge. The scullers moored in the shallows were rapidly sinking, taking in water from holes smashed in their hulls.

Wordlessly, James put his arm about Meirian's shoulders and drew her close to him. Together they watched Lyall sailing further and further away from the island.

'You know what he's going to do, don't you?' muttered James brokenly, unable to take his eyes from his younger brother's progress. 'He's making straight for the devil's tunnel.'

Meirian couldn't speak. She could only watch as Lyall sailed across the expanse of smooth water shining in the morning sunlight like fiery satin. At length, he paused. Lowering himself over the side of the sculler, Lyall raised an arm, and with a confident wave in the direction of Hermitage Island, disappeared from their sight as the soft waters of Swallowhole Mere drew him down and silently closed above him.

'I hope all the old witchcraft tales are true,' mumbled James thickly, burying his face in the softness of Meirian's hair as she wrapped her arms about him and held him tight. 'Whatever he's done, I hope Lyall washes up somewhere safe and sound!'

★ ★ ★

Golden drifts of autumn leaves fluttered past Meirian's window as she buttoned the bodice of her best dress and, turning to the looking-glass, pinned the wedding posy to her collar. Taking the amethyst necklace into her hands, she gazed lost in thought at the mellow sunlight playing upon the ancient gems.

'Meirian,' called James, tapping at her door before entering. 'Ma and Henry are all but ready for the ceremony.'

She glanced around, beaming at him. 'I saw Isabelle earlier; she looks radiant today!'

'I've never seen her happier,' he agreed, adding regretfully, 'If only . . . '

'Lyall could have been here,' finished Meirian gently.

'I like to think he survived and reached the coast, like those long-ago Caunces, and is safe in Italy, painting to his heart's content,' murmured James ruefully. 'He's my brother, Meirian. I miss him.'

'I know.' She squeezed his hand. 'We all do.'

'So are we going downstairs to this wedding?' he went on brightly. 'Rosie, Jonathan and Daisy are all looking very nervous in case the new babe decides to arrive during the ceremony!'

'At least if Baby Petherbridge *does* decide to put in an appearance this afternoon, a doctor will be on hand,' said Meirian with a smile, holding out the necklace for James to admire. 'Wasn't it kind of your mother to give me this to wear at her wedding?'

'Here, let me fasten it for you.' He put it about her neck and closed the heavy gold clasp, bending to touch his lips to her temple. 'It looks well on you, Meirian. Of course, if you want to keep the amethyst necklace, you do realise you'll have to marry me and become the squire's lady?'

Meirian laughed softly, turning within the circle of James's arms and standing on tiptoe to kiss him. 'Oh, I can do that!'

CHRISTMAS AT COORAH CREEK

Janet Gover

English nurse Katie Brooks is spending Christmas at Coorah Creek. She was certain that leaving London was the right decision, but her new job in the outback is more challenging than she ever imagined. Scott Collins rescued her on her first day and has been a source of comfort ever since. But he no longer calls the town home — it's too full of bad memories, and he doesn't plan on sticking around long. Scott needs to leave. Katie needs to stay. They have until Christms to decide their future . . .

THE CHRISTMAS CHOIR

Jo Bartlett

After a chance encounter with a young homeless man, high-flyer Anna reassesses her life. Handing in her notice at her City job, she returns home to St Nicholas Bay. There, she finds that the new vicar is none other than Jamie: the man who severed their relationship when they were teenagers, and took off abroad alone. The pair renew their old acquaintanceship — just as friends. But are the sparks of their long-ago love kindling into life once more?

JESSICA'S CHRISTMAS KISS

Alison May

When Jessica was fifteen, she shared a magical kiss with a mystery boy at a Christmas party. Now almost thirty, she is faced with a less than magical Christmas after uncovering her husband's secret affair. And, whilst she wouldn't admit it, she sometimes finds herself thinking about that perfect Christmas kiss, back when her life still seemed full of hope and possibility. But she never would have guessed that the boy she kissed in the kitchen all those years ago might still think about her too . . .

TWO LOVES

Denise Robins

Bill is handsome, tender and exciting, but Cherry knows she can't live on love alone. Phillip doesn't attract her like Bill does, but his wealth can buy her everything she's always wanted. Cherry is determined to have them both. Cleverly concealing one's existence from the other, she begins leading a dangerous double life, unknowingly pushing all three of them towards disaster . . .

The Forged Coupon